HYDE HOUSE

An Emmie Rose Haunted Mystery Book 3

DEAN RASMUSSEN

DARK VENTURE
PRESS

Hyde House: An Emmie Rose Haunted Mystery Book 3

Dean Rasmussen

For more information about this book, visit:

www.deanrasmussen.com
dean@deanrasmussen.com

Hyde House: An Emmie Rose Haunted Mystery Book 3

Published by:

Dark Venture Press, 601 Central Ave W, Ste 103 #129, Saint Michael, MN 55376

Cover Art: Mibl Art

Developmental & Line Editor: C.B. Moore

❀ Created with Vellum

A lice sat at the dinner table in her white Sunday dress tapping her foot and clutching the pink box. Her stomach fluttered with excitement at the thought of opening her present. How much longer would she need to wait?

Daniel had written "Tiger" across the white ribbon, although the ink had smeared a bit. It didn't matter. What was *inside* mattered.

The birthday cake was on the counter, and she eyed it every few minutes while Ruth prepared the food and Daniel sat across from Alice reading the newspaper.

"Can I open it now?" Alice asked him.

He didn't respond.

Scowling at him, she wadded up her cloth napkin and hurled it into his newspaper. He lowered it with an annoyed expression, staring back at her now, but his gaze was still distant, as if he were deep in thought.

"Did you hear me?" She waved at him. "When can I open it?"

"As soon as we're finished eating." Ruth carried over the roasted chicken and placed it in the center of the table. "A little patience goes a long way."

Alice shook the box. It jingled. "What is it?"

Daniel seemed to snap out of his thoughts and held up his hand. "Don't shake it! It's something to brighten your day. I picked it out myself."

Ruth placed a bowl of soup in front of Alice, stirring it with a spoon as the steam rose out of it. "An appetizer. It's still a little hot."

Alice sat back in her chair. "I don't want soup. I want cake."

"The faster you eat all your food, the faster you'll get what you want."

Alice grumbled. "Who eats soup on their birthday?"

Ruth seemed not to notice and stepped back to the kitchen counter.

"How are you feeling today?" Daniel asked from across the table.

"Better." Alice took a spoonful of soup and gulped it down. She cringed at the taste.

"Is something wrong?" Daniel asked.

"It doesn't taste right."

"Nothing ever tastes right to you, does it?" Daniel said with a smile.

Alice stared at the soup. The steam drifted up and passed over her face. It tasted good, but it needed... something. "Why should Mrs. Syme get every weekend off? Can't she stay with us all the time?"

"She can," Daniel said, "but she has her ailing father to look after as well, and they need time together. Nothing worse than being away from those you love. We shouldn't always rely on others to do everything for us, anyway, should we? Better to take care of things ourselves once in a while. Mom and Dad spoiled us."

"What about Catherine? I hope her father isn't ailing too. Who will take care of me?"

"No need to fret," Ruth said from the counter with a warm smile. "I'm sure Catherine will stay here as long as you need her. I would never abandon you to care for yourself."

Daniel stood grinning and held Ruth in his arms. "And we may need a little more help in the near future, isn't that right? And a little more room?"

Ruth blushed. "Yes, of course, but we have Alice to think about. You know her therapy is costly."

Daniel glanced at Alice, then back at Ruth. "I'll tell her today."

"I think that's best."

"Tell me what?" Alice asked.

"After supper, Tiger. We have more than one surprise in store for you today."

"Splendid!" Alice glanced at her present. It *was* splendid, but just not moving along as splendidly as she'd like. She scratched at the surface of the white ribbon hiding her gift. If the ribbon should break off *accidentally*, no one could blame her for opening the box.

Ruth served Daniel a plate of roast chicken with a blueberry muffin beside it, before serving Alice last. It was always Daniel first, and that was just fine with Alice. Her brother worked hard to manage their parents' business, and he deserved to be treated well. Alice even waited until Daniel took his first bite of chicken before she did the same, not out of any rules of etiquette, but out of respect. But after a bite of chicken, she broke off a piece of her muffin with her fingers and dropped it into her mouth with her head tilted back as Daniel frowned disapprovingly at her.

Ruth finally took her seat next to Daniel. She had a way of making them feel like they were a regular family again, even though nothing felt the same anymore without her parents after they'd died of consumption. They had just gotten sick after coming back from a trip, coughed a lot, then passed away within days of each other. The pain still weighed heavy in her heart, but Ruth had taken over matters concerning the house, and Daniel was off to work most of the time, so any chance to share time together at the table, birthday or not, brightened her day.

"What do you say we go visit Mom and Dad's grave today?" Alice asked.

"Not on your birthday," Ruth said. "Wouldn't you rather spend your time playing?"

"I was just thinking of them. Missing them a little."

"Isn't it enough that you are my favorite sister?" Daniel asked.

"I'm your only sister, rube."

"Alice, don't be crude."

"Sorry."

Daniel winked at her.

Alice took another spoonful of soup. Mrs. Syme's cooking was *way* better than anything Ruth made, but she loved Ruth too much to complain. Nothing had tasted right lately anyway because of Alice's "condition", but Daniel tended to take criticism of Ruth too seriously, so she kept silent.

Ruth and Daniel snuggled, leaning toward each other for a moment at the table. Then Ruth whispered something to Daniel, and he looked at her. He nodded. They looked at Alice with wide smiles.

Daniel could barely contain his grin. "We think it's time to tell you some wonderful news."

Alice swallowed. She didn't like surprises. And they had that look in their eyes.

"We're going to have a baby," Ruth said.

Daniel nodded. "How do you like the title of Aunt Alice?"

Alice's eyes widened, and she smiled, although the concept frightened her. How could she be an aunt? "I'm only fourteen."

Daniel laughed. "You'll do just fine. Are you all right? You look a little stunned."

"I guess. What's its name?"

"We haven't picked out a name yet. I guess it depends on if it's a boy or a girl, right?" Daniel laughed.

"Just don't name her Alice if it's a girl, all right? I want to be the only Alice in this house."

"I promise we won't name her Alice, if it's a girl."

She thought about it some more. "Will I have to take care of it too?"

"You can if you want," Daniel said. "Is that something you'd be comfortable with?"

Alice looked down at her body. The disease had weakened her, though she could still get around just fine, but the thought of helping to take care of a baby overwhelmed her. She preferred quiet solitude to listening to a baby crying. "I hope it won't cry a lot. I can't read with loud noises."

Daniel nodded, still smiling. "I know. I wouldn't worry about it. We won't leave you alone."

"Good. I don't know what I would do if you weren't here with me." Her eyes watered up, and she looked down while trying to cover the sudden surge of emotion. There had been so many changes in the last two years. "I guess it's good for you, and for me too."

Ruth beamed. "I'm sure you'll be a wonderful aunt."

Alice scowled playfully. "Just keep them out of my room."

Daniel frowned. "We'll all do our best."

"Alice," Ruth said, "I'm sure you have nothing to worry about. Changes are scary, but things always work out in the end. You *do* enjoy living with us, don't you? Isn't it nice to share this time together?"

She held up her present. "I *adore* you both, but I want to open my present now."

"Go ahead." Daniel nodded once.

Alice didn't hesitate. She ripped off the bow and lifted the lid to the box. The sparkling beauty of the object inside took her breath away. Something more beautiful than any present she'd received before in her life. A musical jewelry box. Opening it, she searched for anything that might be hidden within it, but the tiny compartments were empty, though her initials were carved into the side. *AH.* It didn't matter that it was empty. She could fill it in no time.

Winding the key along the back, she listened to the music. It played "O Sole Mio," and as the music went on, both Daniel and Ruth urged her to keep eating. She obeyed while staring at the box's intricate workmanship. It was magical, and it calmed her.

When the song finished, she stood up and jumped over to Daniel, pushing away his newspaper and throwing herself into his arms. "It's the best present ever."

"I'm glad you like it, Tiger."

❧ 2 ❧

Emmie extended out her arms over Betty's old possessions as if she would embrace it all, if only she could. "It's a treasure trove."

"It's quite a collection." Sarah looked up from the book she was reading and smiled. "I wish I had more time to read."

Finding out that Betty had a will and had left everything to Emmie had been a big surprise. It wasn't just the monetary value of the house, but the honor and privilege of knowing that Betty had entrusted her precious research, book collection, and artifacts to her.

It was even more surprising considering that Betty hadn't traveled to see Emmie in Green Hills since the old woman had studied her as a child, or made any effort to contact her in any way since her parents had died. The old woman must have felt guilty about the way they'd been killed, bravely facing an evil far too strong for them, and clearly must have thought Emmie was a natural heir to all the knowledge.

But it wasn't like Betty's inheritance would change Emmie's life much—only $7000 in savings—but at least the house was worth something, if Emmie decided to sell. The true wealth lay in the information Betty had compiled over the years, which held incalculable value to her and Sarah, two psychics who had often struggled to understand the depth of their powers, and to Finn, who was eager to decipher all sorts of mysteries related to "the great beyond."

After they first started going through her new possessions, Emmie couldn't help but feel that at any moment someone from Betty's family would arrive to declare the will a mistake. But nobody had disputed anything in the months since the old woman's death. Emmie had signed the papers, accepted the keys, and it had been an adventure discovering such a wealth of information, one-of-a-kind nuggets of occult knowledge in many cases, and some dark secrets that should never be lost to the world. She had silently accepted the responsibility of sorting through everything, categorizing it as much as possible, and finding a safe place for it all, either in her home or at Caine House.

Emmie brushed the hair out of her eyes and stared at the boxes and shelves full of Betty's belongings. It wasn't so bad. She'd done a lot of sorting through accumulated possessions lately, first with her parents' things, and now with Betty's, and they'd already picked through a lot, but the process was slow because after discovering something that interested one of them, they would stop to read or study the item. They were in no rush to go through everything, but at the same time she hungered to learn more about her gift, and so many answers now lay within her grasp.

Sarah had taken a break while Emmie scoured through one of the boxes. Now she held up the book she was reading. "This is some good stuff. I have to try this out."

"What's that?"

"Controlled possession—like what Josephine did to me, except it describes the process through the eyes of the author, an old man with powers like mine. He breaks it down like a medical textbook. Perfect for me. I couldn't quite understand what was happening. It's amazing that there are others out there like us, and people who took the time to write all this down."

"Maybe someday we'll meet some of them." Emmie held up a spiral-bound notebook. "This looks interesting."

"What is it?"

Emmie thumbed through it. "A list of names, addresses, and phone numbers. And judging by some of the names and titles, like priestess and sage and whatnot, I think these people form a sort of... association? Remember the letter from New Orleans that Finn found? The one talking about Josephine?"

"Yeah... The writer was addressing people by high-sounding titles and all."

"Exactly. Like there was a hierarchy. And Betty spoke about something like that, and my parents being part of it. Maybe not the same 'association,' but something or another still exists."

The pages were faded, so some people might be dead or their contact details might be out of date, but she would keep that and maybe copy it into her computer, just in case.

"Maybe one day we'll know how to approach these people." Sarah smiled warmly. "And *who* to approach. And what to ask them."

Emmie returned the smile. Lately, they'd been following each other's train of thought. Sarah didn't need to elaborate on what questions she might ask the people in the notebook. It was understood. Maybe that was due to spending so much time together, or being psychic. Or both.

Finn stepped down the basement stairs, and Emmie slipped away the notebook. If he saw it, he'd go into full journalist mode and start calling people willy-nilly. He appeared carrying an object along with a dusty hardcover book he had found with it. It was a skull wrapped in metal bars, making it look as though it were in a small prison, and it sat on a metal base shaped like a pentagram.

"I couldn't find any matches to light the candles upstairs. Can you believe that?" Finn scoffed. "An occult expert without matches."

"I'm sure there's a box of them around here somewhere." Emmie eyed Finn's discovery. "But what is it?"

He displayed the piece and gestured to the top of the skull where a spike jutted from the bars of the cage. "You need a candle to make this work, apparently. Why do you think Betty kept this around? It's for communicating with the dead."

"I don't need help with that," Emmie rushed to say.

"It's for me."

Emmie held back a response. It was clear that his brother's suicide was still gnawing at the back of his mind.

Finn set the item and book on a small table, then pulled a three-foot-long braid of hair from a box. Both ends were tied with a red ribbon. "What do you suppose this is for?"

"Long hair has always had a connection with spirituality. Maybe it came from a witch?"

Finn studied it and placed it back. "So much stuff on magic, witchcraft, voodoo, and deities. I love it all." He looked around. "I'd always wondered what it might be like to have a stranger leave me something in their will."

"Now you know."

"The books and relics are amazing, but it also would have been useful if she'd left you a larger stash of cash."

"I'd rather have all this."

"Well, yes, I suppose so. By the way, mind if I take some of those statues that Betty collected from overseas?" He gestured to them. "She's got plenty: the Egyptian god Horus, Guan Yin, Chinese goddess of Mercy, Zhong Kui, King of Ghosts, Fudo, Japanese god of Protection, Haitian god Baron Samedi, a loa of the dead..."

Emmie didn't recognize any of the names, but Finn was obviously excited about the prospect of receiving them, so she didn't argue. "You can borrow them, as long as you promise not to release any spirits into the wild."

Sarah fake-coughed. "... Josephine..."

Finn cringed and pressed his hand over his heart. "Ouch."

Emmie chuckled. They hadn't stopped reminding him of his crush on an alluring ghost.

He inspected the metal door at the back of the basement where Emmie had been trapped a couple of months earlier during her confrontation with Josephine. "Who do you suppose built this room?"

"Since Betty wasn't living here that long, I'm guessing the previous owners built it. They built the house in the fifties, so maybe it was a nuclear bunker-type room. Many people had them back then."

"I suppose. Hey, I've got an idea."

"No!" Sarah laughed.

"Hear me out. Since I'm living at Caine House now, and you have this place right up the road from me, wouldn't it be great to sell Hanging House and move in here?"

"You keep pressuring me to move out of there. I think you just want us to live here so you can flirt with the *girls next door*." Emmie swayed her hips.

Finn grinned. "Something like that. This isn't the greatest house, but I would love to have you two for neighbors. And really, not for your cooking."

"Alice would miss me too much," Emmie said. "And I'm not sure Hanging House would be so easy to sell at this point. It still needs a lot of work. I still have those same electrical problems to fix and everyone in town still remembers that it's an old haunted house. Plenty of neighbors would rather see me tear it down than sell it."

"Think about it, at least." Finn walked over and looked through the books that Sarah had been stacking next to her. "What have you got there?" He picked up a thick hardcover on merging with spirits and automatic writing. "That sounds interesting. Isn't merging with spirits pretty much the same thing as a possession?"

"No. Not really," she said eagerly. "Possessions are focused mostly on demons violently taking over someone else. Merging is opening yourself up to the will of another without losing your own will. It's like working together, sharing your space, a loving act."

Finn listened attentively while Sarah spoke. He was good at that because of his natural curiosity, although he didn't have a lot of patience for everyday things. When Sarah went back to her reading, he looked through a stack of books a few feet away and picked one out. "Do you know what I could use?"

"What?"

"This." He held up a book on love and romance spells. "I'm a committed amateur and could become an expert." As Sarah stood to stretch, he threw his arms around her. "You said before we could keep whatever we got a hold of, Emmie, so I'm keeping her."

Sarah squirmed within his grasp, but she was smiling. "I'm not for keeps." She pushed his arm away and stepped aside.

"I wouldn't try those spells on Sarah, if I were you," Emmie said. "She'll hex you."

"I'm up for that," he said with another grin. "Especially if it makes me do whatever she wants."

Sarah snorted, blushing.

Emmie rolled her eyes. "Something tells me you might regret that. And no, you can't have that particular book. You could do a lot of damage. Remember what happened with—"

"You're not going to say—"

"Josephine," Sarah said.

Emmie nodded. "It's true."

"Oh God, where is the book on erasing someone's memory?"

Sarah tapped the stack of books next to her. "What do you say if we break for lunch now and head back to the house with the stuff we sorted today?"

Emmie laughed. "I'd rather just keep reading, but you mortals need sustenance, I understand."

"So that's how you feel about us now." Finn smirked.

"Well, do you own two houses?"

"Touché, Miss Em."

They left Betty's house with plenty of material to study and arrived back at Hanging House nearly an hour later. Pulling into the driveway, Emmie spotted the outside house lights flickering on and off. Then she noticed that even the inside lights were doing the same thing. The same random electrical problems she'd seen most of her life in the house. And they appeared to be getting worse.

They waited for Finn to come up next to them, carrying most of the stuff. "Alice must be upset," he said.

"I need to get the wiring fixed one of these days. It's been going on for so long that I don't think about it anymore. One day, the whole thing will burn down."

"Leave them like that, at least until after Halloween is over. The trick-or-treaters would love it. They'd think it was special effects."

"Most kids don't dare to come to this house on Halloween. Except for a group of teenagers who show up every year to ring the doorbell on a dare and run off."

"Maybe we should have a little fun with them this year, you know? I'll stand in the window with a white sheet over me, then you jump out from around the side of the house."

Sarah laughed. "Please, let's put up decorations, at least?"

Finn nodded. "I'm in."

"Alice would get upset at all the disruption. And that's the last thing I want right now."

Sarah looked at Emmie curiously. "I guess you have no love for this holiday. But haven't you *ever* gone trick-or-treating?"

"Once, and it was fun for a little while. I went with a group of friends when I was about ten. I even mistakenly thought one of the boys, who was wearing a zombie outfit, was a real dead child. He tried talking with me, but I ignored him, thinking he was dead, you know, because he looked like a *real* dead kid. That pissed him off, so he called me a bunch of awful names and harassed me, which spoiled the entire night."

"Oh, but now you can tell which is which." Sarah leaned into Emmie. "Maybe it would be fun."

"We'll see." Emmie looked up at her house. It was still a *haunted* house.

Finn gestured to the wavering light streaming out of the windows as they moved over the lawn. "It's getting worse," he said. "I know Alice is moody, but you might truly have a problem. There are some tools in my trunk, so I'll have a look at it. I know enough to fix this sort of thing, at least until a professional can get to it."

The lights kept flickering on and off as they walked to the front door. Emmie tried to remember anything she might have done earlier that morning to upset Alice, but nothing came to mind.

"Just don't agitate Alice any more than you have to, Finn."

"I got this."

※ 3 ※

S arah felt the anger in the room as soon as she stepped inside. The lights flickered on and off as the three of them made their way into the living room.

"Alice?" Emmie called out, then turned to Sarah. "Do you see her?"

The question caught Sarah off guard, and her first impulse was to shake her head—of course, Sarah couldn't see Alice—but they had been trying something new lately. A technique she had picked up from one of Betty's books, to focus on a spirit's "aura," and in particular Alice's emotional aura, which began appearing recently as shifting colors in the air, sometimes flaring and vanishing, depending on the girl's state of mind. Sarah squinted across the room and focused her eyesight and mind. "Not yet."

Staring into the emptiness still seemed odd, but working together with Emmie, Sarah had gotten better at it. She'd described the auras to Emmie as "vibrant rainbows," and the forms would appear if she followed the book's advice—an intuitive process of seeing with her heart, rather than her eyes. It had come easier in the last few days, so Alice's form appeared nearly complete. Sarah could now even hear Alice's voice, although it was distant and soft, but if she quieted her mind and focused, Alice's presence and voice manifested in the room, just as Betty's books had suggested they could.

Betty's words came back to her: *You two together can be dangerous. Like a chemical reaction. If you learn to use the combination, it's gold.*

A few times, Sarah had regretted picking up that new skill, like during some of Alice's tantrums and even when the girl walked through the house late at night for no reason, but mostly it wasn't so bad. At least Alice only appeared as a form of light, and not the full, physical presence that had terrorized Emmie's childhood. But being able to communicate with Alice's spirit had helped them grow closer.

Finn stepped toward the kitchen. "I'll go look at that wiring now."

"Don't want a drink first?" Emmie asked.

"I better wait until after."

Emmie nodded. "You know where to go?"

"I got it."

As she put down her box, Sarah looked at the book on top of the stack inside hers. *Embodied Enlightenment: Communication with the Afterlife.* It was a subject Emmie had studied a lot lately, especially given the increase in her abilities to see adult spirits, but Sarah could benefit from studying it too. The better they could interact with the spirits, the more they could help.

Something moved at the edge of Sarah's perception. She turned and spotted Alice watching them from the doorway to her own apartment at the back of the house. "Alice is here."

Emmie looked over. "Did we disturb you?" she asked the ghost.

Alice didn't answer. Her aural outline was grayer than usual, and the slender tones wavered in and out of existence. Sarah sensed a torrent of sadness and a lot more frustration than usual.

Sarah walked over to her and had to follow her into the apartment. "Is something wrong?"

"Where is Daniel?"

"Who's Daniel?"

"My brother. When you were gone today, I remembered that he should have been back by now."

Sarah paused to think for a moment. She had read something about Alice having a brother, but didn't remember the details. "I'm not sure where he is."

The small voice said, "I'm fine with having you here, but when Daniel returns, you'll need to leave. And it'll be soon."

Sarah's eyes widened. This was something she would definitely need to tell Emmie about.

Alice seemed a little more upset. "It's been a long time since they've been gone. Catherine never leaves me alone this long." Alice scowled.

"Who's Catherine?"

"Don't be such a rube."

Sarah looked into Alice's face now, dimly making out the bulging eyes and the permanent grin that came with a scowl which Emmie had so often described. Alice's aura moved over to the window. "Where are they? They shouldn't be gone this long."

"Did they leave you at home alone?"

"Of course not. Daniel wouldn't do such a thing. He always watches out for me. He made sure that I have someone who takes care of me because of the treatments."

Sarah straightened up. "What treatments?"

"All the stuff that Catherine needs to do. Why can't they just leave me alone and let me go outside and play with the other kids?"

"Can't you do that now?"

"They won't let me."

"Who won't let you?"

"Everyone."

"Why do they say you can't go outside?"

"It's too dangerous. *It's for your own good,*" Alice mocked.

Having seen so many patients over the years, it was only natural that Sarah tried to guess what treatments "Catherine" might have tried on the girl. There were a few clues in Alice's appearance that might reveal the truth. Her bulging eyes and gaunt appearance were symptomatic of any number of diseases.

"Alice, do you get tired easily?"

"Why?"

"Maybe I can help diagnose your illness. I'm a nurse, too, remember?"

"I remember. No, I don't feel tired all the time."

"What about severe headaches? Do your head and neck hurt?"

"Sometimes."

"And about the treatments that Catherine gives you, what are those for?"

Alice shrugged. "My condition." She growled. "I don't know. I'm not a doctor. It makes everything so awful. I can't play with the other children. I'm tired all the time, and even my food tastes so strange. Why are you asking me so many questions?"

Sarah chuckled to ease the tension. "I guess it's not important right now. Let's forget about everything for a little while." Sarah sat at the small two-seat table beneath the window looking out over the back lawn. "Did you have any hobbies? Play any instruments or things like that?"

"Not really, but I listen to music as much as I can. I've never tried to play an instrument, although I sit at your piano sometimes when you're gone and hit the keys, but my fingers don't seem to make the right sounds."

Sarah remembered some of the things she had read lately regarding automatic writing and allowing a spirit to take over a body and control it. The spirit could then express itself in a more direct method. She had learned the hard way that this was possible through her previous encounters with Josephine, but the literature explained how it was beneficial for both parties, if done correctly.

"Would you like to try something?" Sarah asked.

Alice met Sarah's gaze. "Like what?"

"I don't know if this will work, but would you like to try to play the piano with me? I could teach you a few things, I think."

After a moment, Alice said, "You would laugh."

"No, I wouldn't."

"I don't feel like playing the piano right now, anyway."

Sarah looked at the piano, then around the room, searching for anything she might use to help distract Alice. "Is there anything else you like to do? Just for fun?"

"I like to write poetry sometimes."

"Okay." Sarah looked at a notepad on the table and a pen next to it. "Let's try that."

"What?"

"Come over here and stand beside me. Let's write poetry together."

Alice sighed as if giving in, but sauntered over to Sarah's side.

Sarah gestured with her head. "Come in really close, right up to me."

Alice moved in closer, and although her spirit was cold and her emotions full of frustration, Sarah allowed it to pass through her a little.

"Put your hand over mine and we'll write the poetry together." Alice's hand sat above Sarah's until it sank in and merged. It was an icy sensation, a tingling like someone pressing a cold compress against her skin. Uncomfortable at first, but not unbearable. Sarah felt the girl's curiosity and wonder at the unfamiliar sensation. Her muscles flexed and relaxed before she clutched the pen involuntarily. "All right, now use my pen to write something."

"You won't laugh?"

"I promise I won't laugh."

Alice's spirit tugged on Sarah's hand and the sensations were similar to the forceful takeover by Josephine, but now it was a serene experience, almost playful. Sarah allowed Alice to write out the first words.

Dear brother, come back soon and get these rubes out of my house.
Alice laughed.

Sarah's heart beat faster and she grinned, staring with amazement at what she'd just written... or rather, what *Alice* had written. The girl had written in cursive, something Sarah hadn't done since junior high school, and the style was completely different from her own. *This is Alice's handwriting, and... it worked! A new skill. I can't wait to tell Emmie about this.* She held back her excitement and glanced at Alice. "That doesn't sound like poetry to me."

"You wanted me to try it."

"How about something a little more *poetic?*"

"Fine." Alice paused for a few seconds, then started again.

When you are away, darkness fills my day. How can I be strong when you've been away for too long?

Sarah read the lines, though she'd technically written them. "That's more like it. That's very good."

"Can you send this to him? Tell him that I miss him?"

Sarah felt the sadness well up in Alice, with her spirit moving in and out of her body. The girl's sadness grew darker and colder the longer she stood there. Sarah shifted in her seat to move out of Alice's space. It was getting too chilly. "Let's see if we can try something else."

Alice backed away and turned to face the open threshold leading toward the front door. "Where is he?" Her aura flared bright red and orange. She stomped her foot. "Tell him to get back here right *now!*"

The lights flickered and then went out.

❧ 4 ❧

Finn stepped down the stairs to the basement. The walls bore the marks from when Alice had attacked him with his own tripod during his first encounter in the house. Those memories were vivid in his mind, and a little anxiety still shot through him, although he knew nothing like that would happen again... At least, *probably* not. Alice, he'd learned, was a temperamental girl, and he needed to exhibit a little extra care when dealing with her.

Once bitten, twice shy, and he intended to treat her with kid gloves. But whether or not Alice's temperament had something to do with the malfunctioning lights, something was messed up down there. Maybe he couldn't fix it, but he could claim a victory by narrowing down the cause.

The lights flickered even as he reached the bottom of the stairs. He had grabbed a flashlight from the kitchen on the way down, just in case the power shut off completely, and now he switched it on in advance, avoiding the necessary adjustment to the sudden flashes of light and dark.

Turning right at the bottom of the stairs into the laundry room, he found the circuit breaker and checked all the fuses. The box itself was very outdated. A sticker on the front had the name of the electrical business that had serviced it the last time, giving a phone number and a date when to get the next inspection done. It was doubtful that someone had ever serviced it since then.

The wiring wasn't frayed or exposed as far as he could see, but he followed the main line across the ceiling. There were no ceiling panels to obscure the beams and floorboards, so following the wiring wasn't terribly difficult. He encountered plenty of spiders along the way as he continued following the line as far as he could. One of the lines led him back into the far corner of the basement beneath Sarah's apartment, to the room where Emmie's dad, Finn recalled, had once set up his office to study the occult. No signs that anything "dark" had occurred there. The room was bare, except for a couple of shelves bolted to the walls.

The line ended near the ceiling and dropped behind a brick wall.

No issues.

He was returning to the beginning of the line, where it first branched off near the circuit breaker, but glanced back before leaving the room and saw the light glint off the wiring.

Shielded wiring didn't glint.

He studied the walls. The two outer walls were lined with red brick, but directly beneath the electrical line, a patch of brick didn't quite match all the others. It was a larger section, about three feet wide by three feet high, and at the very edge of where the wire and the wall met, something had stripped away the plastic shielding.

Not a big deal unless the exposed wires continued behind the wall, but there was no way to know without...

Ripping the damn thing out.

He calculated the amount of work needed to rip down the bricks to get to the wiring. His back hurt already. He could leave the work to a professional, but he wasn't about to put the burden on Emmie unless he absolutely had to.

Examining the wiring again, he cringed. So dangerous. Why had the previous owners left it exposed all these years? It was true that the house had stayed empty and unsold for a while, and perhaps Emmie's parents had not wanted strangers down here? They seemed the sort to have worried more about a bonfire in another plane of existence than an actual one burning down their house.

Finn stepped out of the room and shouted toward the ceiling, "I think I found the problem."

No response.

He examined the mismatched wall section and found a few cracks. If the basement had leaked water into the cracks and had touched the wiring beneath it, that could explain the electrical problems. Maybe someone had patched up the wall after fixing a previous water-damage incident and they hadn't done such a great job, stripping away some of the wiring.

Only one way to tell. Open it up again and follow the line down.

The wiring also was very close to the wood. Amazing that it hadn't already started a fire. He ran his fingers across the cracks in the brick, now aware that if the bricks were touching the wire, he might electrocute himself.

Be careful, Finn. Emmie's voice echoed in his mind. He would catch hell from her if he injured himself. He backed away, then plodded back to the bottom of the stairs and called up, "Shutting off the power!"

"Okay," Emmie's voice came back.

He went to the circuit panel and switched off all the power in the house.

Ready to go.

Now there was only the problem of opening up the wall. He hadn't brought a lot of tools with him, just the usual items found in his trunk in case of an emergency, but he rejoiced at seeing a crowbar lying beneath one leg of the washer. Emmie had put it there, Finn remembered, to keep the washer from rattling during a load because of the uneven floor.

Using the flashlight to find it, Finn pulled out the crowbar from under the washer and walked back to the corner room, slapping the tool into his hands like a gangster ready to do a little damage. Should he ask Emmie before breaking apart her wall? What was the point? An electrician would charge a fortune, so he was really doing her a favor by just getting it over with. Always better to ask forgiveness than permission, anyway.

Returning to the wall, he ran his fingers over the cracks and along the edge of the bricks near the wiring, looking for any places to get some leverage. He jammed the hooked end of the crowbar into a crack he found along the top and thrust it upward. The old, mismatched bricks cracked and broke away after a lot of effort. Whoever had patched it up originally had done a thorough job. The ones along the top kicked up some dust and several dead spiders and bugs dropped on him, followed by the first brick. He worked up a sweat within minutes and expected Emmie or Sarah to come running down in a panic at any moment to yell, "What the hell are you doing?" But they never appeared, despite all the noise.

It would take him longer than expected.

Working his way down, he opened up an area similar in size to the mismatched bricks and discovered a hole behind the wall. He didn't stop to look inside, even as the hole became larger. As he moved down, a section of electrical wiring dangled within the shadows just inside the hole. Following the cable across, he found it led straight to an outlet near the floor. The shielding over the wiring was nearly all stripped away.

No reason to do more demo at this point. The wiring problems were obvious. He pulled on the wire for a moment, following it with his flashlight back into the darkness. Something was in there. A pile of old clothes? The wire wound behind it.

That's different.

He reached in and touched the lace trim of a dress, then ran his fingers across an old coat.

Pulling on the fabric, he felt something weighing it down. The mass shifted within the hole and turned toward him. A subtle crack came from deep within the object, then another. It had to be discarded clothing or debris someone had used as a cheap fix to fill in the hole. As he clutched the fabric more tightly, a piece of it tore away, and his fingernails scratched along the smooth surface of something solid, like the leg of an antique chair.

Stirring up some dust and stale air, he winced and yanked his hand away, then focused the light on where it had ripped. Further into the darkness, he stopped on what he thought was the matted fur of a dead animal. A large raccoon or a dog? He reached in again and pushed it onto its side. Not fur—hair. And there was a skull attached to it tilted away, almost perpendicular to the body.

The face of a long-dead woman looked back at him.

He choked on a cry and couldn't breathe. It didn't look real. She looked like a prop from a horror movie, but the withered, leathery flesh clung to her skeleton as if something had sucked all her innards out. Long strands of braided hair still draped down over her back. She was crumpled up in the small space as if someone had hastily stuffed her in there. He stumbled back and caught his breath as he set the crowbar on the floor.

He had seen so much death, both from working with Emmie and from his job as a journalist covering crime scenes, but this churned his stomach. Nausea swept up, and he forced himself to look away so as not to vomit.

Without looking back, he walked to the bottom of the stairs and took a few deep breaths before calling up to the girls. "Emmie, Sarah, I found your electrical problem. You guys need to come down here now!" Another deep breath. "Bring an extra flashlight... and a barf bag."

E mmie smelled something was *off* as she walked with Sarah over to the room where Emmie's father had set up his occult office years earlier. Not a foul smell, but a distinct odor in the air that struck her as *not quite right*.

Finn stood outside the door with his arms crossed over his chest. He wasn't grinning.

She glanced at Sarah along the way to comment on Finn's appearance, but instead focused on Sarah's pale face, and she wasn't her usual cheerful self, either. "Are you feeling okay?"

Sarah stared across the basement at Finn. "What is it, Finn?" she asked faintly.

Emmie's gaze returned to Finn. "What happened?"

He gestured at the room's open doorway but made no comment.

From the door they could see the brick wall he'd torn away, exposing a gaping hole. She swallowed and expected Finn to give her the bad news, that her electrical problem was far worse than he'd thought, and judging by the damage so far, she couldn't help but wonder how much it would cost to repair. But even before Finn spoke, she spotted the soiled clothes in the hole that formed the outline of a woman crouched in a fetal position. She followed the contours of the arms and legs and then the head, which was bent off to the side, almost buried beneath the lace garments and long, matted dark brown hair.

"Oh, my God." Emmie gasped.

Sarah let out a sympathetic moan, then moved in a little closer. "Who is she?"

"That's my first question," Emmie answered.

"Where was Alice buried?" Finn asked. "Maybe it's her."

"No. She's at the cemetery. I've visited her grave a few times, out of curiosity."

"Well, either someone didn't get a proper burial, or we have a bigger problem."

Emmie moved closer, leaned in, and studied the woman's face as much as she could without gagging. The woman had obviously been there a very long time, judging by her clothes. She was wearing a frilly white dress as if prepared for some formal event, and her emaciated legs led down to her feet still stuck inside her black dress shoes. The woman's hands were folded in her lap, with her fingers curled in and tangled as if she'd been praying in her final moments.

"I think it's quite obviously murder," Finn said. "Whoever put her here did it in a hurry by the way she's just stuffed into that space."

"I don't think we were meant to find her," Sarah said.

"We'll need to call John," Emmie said. "I wonder if he'll be surprised after all that's happened in this house."

Finn looked at her with concern.

Sarah met Emmie's gaze. "Do you think someone murdered her? Do you see a spirit?"

Emmie glanced around the room, then shook her head. "No. Maybe she was murdered somewhere else and then brought back here?"

"But you couldn't see adult spirits until recently anyway," Finn said, "so maybe she was here the whole time and is still here."

"Maybe..." Emmie took a deep breath and tried not to look haunted.

"Or remember all the trouble we had at Caine House where neither of you could see the spirits because of the occult magic?" Finn went on. "Do you think it might be something like that with her?"

"I'm not sure. It's possible." Gathering her courage, Emmie reached in and touched the woman's sleeve. Dry and dirty, yet she felt nothing beyond the fabric.

"The only strong emotions I feel here are coming from Alice upstairs," Sarah said.

The dead woman's mouth hung open as if frozen in her last cry for help. Twisted within the dress, leathery skin held back protruding bones like a finger poking against a sheet of latex. Despite the decay, she was remarkably well preserved, and judging by her hair and clothing style, she was a young rural woman from the early twentieth century.

"It's so strange that she's been here all along," Emmie said. "I wonder if my mom and dad knew something about this?"

"Given their fascination with the occult, wouldn't they have dug her up if they did?" Finn used his foot to move aside a fallen brick on the floor.

"You're right. They would have forced me to communicate with her, if they'd known. I'm guessing she was put in the wall soon after the house was built, judging from the style of her clothes, but that would mean that Alice's brother Daniel and his wife Ruth were living here when it happened."

"Maybe this is what triggered Alice's frustration with Daniel?" Sarah said. "I can still feel her pain from down here, like waves of sadness."

"Yeah, you don't look so good." Finn put his hand on her forehead. "You're cold."

Sarah nodded. "The curse of an empath. I wonder if she knows anything about this, but I'm afraid to ask."

"Why?" Finn asked. "Maybe that's the best way to confirm the woman's identity."

"Alice might get more upset if she knows her." Emmie scanned the mess on the floor. "Better not bring it up, at least for now."

"So if this isn't Alice, then maybe it's Ruth?" Finn said. "How old was she when she died? And where was she buried?"

"I don't know," Emmie said. "I haven't done that much research on them."

Finn focused his light on the woman again. "Maybe this is her."

"Do you think Daniel could have done this?" Sarah asked. "Sold the house, killed his wife and gone on to live it up somewhere else? I mean, when wives are killed, look at the husband. Right?"

"Men are monsters," Finn said, nodding sarcastically.

"I think that's a question for Alice, if we manage to put it to her." Emmie winced. "But we should get Sarah outside, away from Alice for a bit, and get John over here so he can take a look. We have to call the police, anyway."

Now past the initial shock, Emmie took Finn's flashlight and leaned into the hole while scanning the area behind the woman. The wall only extended back a few inches beyond the body—obviously it was constructed for the sole purpose of hiding the woman —but something in the dirt near the woman's waist caught her eye. It was a small cloth object, about the size of her hand, and it resembled a stick figure a child might create with a craft kit. The flashlight showed there was a clump of hair attached to the doll, the same color and texture as the woman's, and a generic face and limbs.

"This looks occult to me," Emmie said. "Do you see it?"

Finn leaned in and focused his own light on the object. "I didn't see that before. What's with its mouth?"

Tiny threads zigzagged over the doll's mouth, effectively sewing it shut.

"Do you think that was done to silence her?" Emmie turned to Finn.

"That's my first impression, from what I know of voodoo, but what's it doing *here?*"

Emmie shrugged. "That would explain why I never heard anything from her before, if that's how it works."

She reached in and plucked the doll out of the dirt beside the woman. As soon as she disturbed the doll, a wisp of smoke filled the room, followed by a muffled scream that surrounded them. An apparition formed, the shadowy figure of a woman, and circled in the air overhead before it rushed out of the room. It stood briefly outside the door before racing away in a burst of light, even as the muted cries continued.

Still clutching the doll, Emmie charged out of the room after the woman, followed by Sarah and Finn. The woman's subdued cries of pain led them up to the main floor, but within a minute, she had disappeared.

They continued searching through every room of the house as fast as they could, hoping for a chance to communicate with her, but finally gave up and gathered in the living room, each of them out of breath.

"We lost her," Sarah said.

"Listen," Finn said, gesturing to the doll still in Emmie's hand, "can we take a moment and all agree it wasn't my fault this time?"

❦ 6 ❧

The spirit from the basement had disappeared, but maybe Alice could identify her.

Finn pronounced it safe to turn on the lights again, and on the way to the apartment, Emmie stopped and looked back at him. "You should wait here while we talk to her. Nothing personal."

"I understand. Women-understand-women type of thing, right?" He smirked.

Sarah exaggerated a return smirk. "I'm glad you understand."

Emmie led Sarah back into the apartment area and called out for Alice. The girl appeared, although her expression was anything but delightful. Her twisted frown and gaze lacked any enthusiasm, and she was mumbling with her hands curled into fists.

"Alice?" Emmie asked. "You okay?"

Alice looked confused and barely acknowledged her.

Sarah leaned toward Emmie. "She's upset because Daniel hasn't come back yet."

Alice glared at them, and the frustration on her face was clear. "Where is he?"

"I'm not sure, but we'll try to help you find him."

Alice went back to grumbling as she turned away from them, glancing over her shoulder every few seconds toward the front door.

"Can you help us?" Emmie asked. "There's a woman in the basement, and she needs us."

This seemed to grab Alice's attention. She looked into Emmie's eyes. "Who?"

"We don't know her name. That's what we wanted to ask: Maybe you know her?"

A puzzled look spread over Alice's face. "What's she doing down there?"

Sarah cleared her throat and met Emmie's gaze before speaking. "I'm afraid it looks like... she died. Do you know anything about it?"

Alice's expression transformed into an angry cringe as if insulted by the question. "Why would I know anything about dead bodies?"

Emmie smiled as best she could. "She needs a proper burial."

Alice huffed, then spoke softly. "I don't know who it is."

Emmie raised her voice while pleading, "Would you mind coming down to look at her?"

"I don't want to see dead people! What's wrong with you? I want my brother."

Emmie took a deep breath. Pressuring Alice wasn't going to help, so she softened her voice and focused on what was important to Alice at the moment. Maybe by acknowledging her current obsession, they might wrangle the identity of the murdered woman out of her. "Where did he go?"

"Where do you think he went? It's Sunday. Everyone goes to church on Sunday."

"You didn't go with them?"

She grumbled. "I don't need to go to their stupid church."

"Okay. Did Daniel and Ruth have a fight lately?"

Alice narrowed her eyes. "What do you mean?"

"I mean, did they argue? Before church or... in general?"

Her scowl was growing. "About what?"

"I don't know. Money? Life? Or... love? Did he... get angry at her?"

Alice erupted in anger and shouted, "What are you talking about? My brother is the most wonderful man in the world. I don't like the way you're talking about him. Not at all. I love Daniel, and Ruth loves Daniel too. Everybody loves Daniel. He takes good care of me, and as soon as he gets back, I might tell him what you said."

"I'm sorry, Alice, that came out wrong. I'm just trying to find out more about your brother."

"He is wonderful, but not so nice to rubes who ask stupid questions. You better not say anything mean about my brother." Alice's face contorted at the verge of rage. Emmie hadn't seen that face since she was a child. Still, Alice was the only person who might be able to answer their questions about the mysterious body.

Emmie forced herself to smile and spoke more softly. "It's just hard to think right now because of the woman downstairs, that's all."

"Nobody... died... in my... house." After that statement, said in decisive tones, Alice simply vanished.

That had never happened before. Emmie glanced at Sarah. "Is she...?"

Sarah nodded. "She's gone. I can see her better now. I think merging with her helped a little, but she's so upset about her brother."

"Merging...?"

Finn poked his head in the open doorway. "Sorry, I was eavesdropping and I'm only hearing one side of the conversation, but I take it we are going in circles and not getting any answers?"

Shrugging, Sarah moved toward him. "It's okay. She just left, anyway."

"Let's adjourn to our office, then," Finn said, leading the way to the kitchen and taking his usual spot at the table. He had laid out a bowl with chips and something that looked like guacamole. "Tell me all about it."

"She keeps talking about her brother." Emmie sat next to him and grabbed a chip which she dipped in the avocado.

Sarah got three beers out of the fridge and sat opposite Emmie. "Keeps saying how wonderful he is."

"Interesting," Finn said, taking his bottle. "So she keeps insisting on this now and before didn't talk so much about him? Because she might have sensed something about the dead body about to be discovered, and she is really into denial, this poor girl. If this Daniel guy did kill his wife, then she might know, deep down. If she was a ghost in the house she might even have witnessed it and have scrubbed it out of her memory."

Alice appeared, crouched on the table right in front of Finn. Her face had contorted into a nightmarish mess as she screamed in his face, "You liar! You can't say that about my brother. I'll kill you!"

Emmie and Sarah gasped as Alice sliced her hand through his neck.

Busy opening his beer, Finn shivered, then looked up in surprise with wide eyes, oblivious to the ghost he couldn't see, and a fury he couldn't feel.

Alice turned to Emmie and Sarah. "I let you all come into my house and live with me, and then you say horrible things about my brother, but he never hurts anyone. He'll be back soon, and when he is, then maybe he'll kick you all out on the street after what you said about him. Maybe he will kill you. And I won't stop him."

The lights flickered wildly, and Finn glanced up toward the ceiling. "Was it something I said?"

Emmie reached out to Alice. "Please, Alice. Our friend didn't mean anything by it."

"He's just being silly," Sarah added.

"I hate him!" Her eyes bulged and her fingers curled into

claws, and for the first time in a long time Emmie was afraid of what the girl might do.

Finn sat still, his gaze jumping from Emmie, then to Sarah.

Then, just as abruptly as she had appeared, Alice was gone again.

Sarah glanced around the kitchen, then went to the fridge and pulled off a magnetic notepad. Writing something as she returned to the table, she showed it to them. *Earlier, she said something about the metallic taste in her food. Poison?*

Finn gave a low whistle. "That would be truly monstrous."

Emmie took the pen from Sarah, shielding what she was writing. *If Daniel had something to do with the woman in the basement, and maybe even Alice's death, we shouldn't talk about it around her.*

"Agreed." Sarah nodded.

"You know, I can see you acting sneaky," Alice's voice erupted directly behind Emmie.

Emmie turned around. Alice stood inches away, but her anger had cooled now.

"Please don't be mad, Alice. We're only trying to figure out what happened to the dead woman. She needs our help."

"Then figure it out without saying mean things about my brother, or you won't see me again."

An icy chill filled the room and once again Alice disappeared.

7

John arrived a short time later, still dressed in his police uniform. Wielding his baton-sized police flashlight, he walked in and glanced around. "So let me have a look at this woman you found."

"You won't believe where we found her. In my dad's old office back in the far corner." Emmie led him through the kitchen and down the stairs to the basement. Finn and Sarah followed closely.

"I never went down there much," John said.

She took him to the hole and moved out of the way so John could have a clear view of the woman.

Shining the flashlight into the corpse's face, he grunted and nodded as if it wasn't any big surprise. He examined the skeleton, moving closer to it than any of them had gotten, but left her untouched for the most part, only poking around a little with his flashlight.

"That's a corpse, all right. I was hoping you might be wrong about this. You know, sometimes people find strange things hidden away in old houses, dolls and mannequins, and every once in a while I get a call to investigate a dead baby only to find out when I get there that it's just a doll some kid left behind. It happens more than you think."

"What should we do?" Emmie asked.

"Don't mess with it."

"Too late." Finn held out the voodoo artifact. "We found this with the body."

John examined it, turning it over with a puzzled look. "This is a strange thing to discover in Green Hills." He looked at Emmie. "Something your parents might have collected."

"I agree."

"But I can see they couldn't have had anything to do with it. If you found it with her, it's been there since she died." There was relief and worry on Finn's face as John pulled out a plastic bag from his pocket and slipped the doll inside.

"What now?" Emmie asked.

"Well, we obviously can't leave her like this. I'll contact the Medical Examiner's Office and see if we can't get this body removed today." John turned to Finn. "I recommend you keep this quiet. No Internet articles about this one, got it? This poor girl"—he put a hand on Emmie's shoulder—"has already been through enough in this house, and she doesn't need any more publicity of this nature."

"No problem. Not a word out of me. My mouth is..." Finn gestured toward the doll while making the zipper gesture over his lips.

John still studied him closely. "May I ask why you were ripping a hole in the wall in the first place?"

"We were trying to solve her electrical problem." Finn had a guilty look.

"He was helping me find the source of the problems." Emmie gestured to the frayed wires hanging down over the hole running next to the body. "Looks like he was onto something."

John looked at the wires, then back at Finn. "You an electrician?"

"No, sir," Finn said.

"Then why the hell are you messing around with old wiring like this, even if you are doing it as a favor for her? A professional should fix this, not a *ghost hunter*." John turned to Emmie. "I'll get someone over here today, if possible, to have a look at your wiring, but we'll take care of the body first. I'm sorry, I knew about the problems a while ago, but I guess I didn't understand the extent of the issue. I should have had someone fix this before you moved in."

"It's okay. You did a lot for me already, and I know it's expensive to fix."

"It might take the authorities a few hours to remove the body, but you should stick around to answer questions, although I doubt there will be an investigation, given the fact that maybe a hundred years have passed. They don't usually do an autopsy in a situation like this, and the murderer would be dead by now."

"No money to look into vintage cases, huh?" Finn asked.

John turned his flashlight on Finn, who squeezed his eyes shut. A silence passed between them until John focused the flashlight on the woman's face again.

"I'll make some calls now." John stepped out of the room, and they followed him upstairs. "It won't take the coroner long to get here, but we will have to make a report of how you found her. Just going through procedure, nothing to worry about." He told Finn, "Make sure you stick around too."

Passing through the kitchen, he paused near the front door, took out his phone, and scanned his flashlight over the books in the living room.

"Looks like some unusual reads there."

"Probably nothing you'd be interested in."

"Not in this stash," John agreed, shaking his head. He turned his attention to the walls and ceiling. "I know we talked about this, but you don't need to stay in this house. Maybe that old woman's house you inherited would be a better place for you. You can see all the problems you're going to face here. Maybe it's better to step away and let someone else take care of it."

"You're probably right, but I'm not ready to leave quite yet, and it would still be difficult to sell."

He indicated the books with his chin. "You know, these books might seem entertaining, but there's no need to hang on to the past. Just because your parents liked that stuff, doesn't mean you need to go down the same path."

"I definitely won't go down that same path, but everyone likes a good mystery, right?"

John smiled warmly. "You always were a bit stubborn. That's probably one of the reasons I like you. Just remember that you've got an obligation to yourself, too. Mental health is just as important as the physical."

"You're right, again."

"That's..." John stopped.

The sound of a girl's laughter came from upstairs. Emmie glanced up toward the sound, recognizing it as Alice's voice, but she had never heard Alice laugh before—not *ever*. She would go up there to check on her, but not while John was around.

Now John aimed his flashlight at the doorway leading up. "What's that?"

Emmie thought only she had heard the laughter. "What?"

"Is someone up there?"

"Oh, I probably have the old battery-powered radio on, the one I took from Betty's house."

John seemed to accept her answer but kept his gaze on the stairway for a few seconds longer before making a call on his phone and turning away to speak.

Finn moved them off to the side where he leaned in closer to Emmie, while keeping an eye on John at the same time. "You know, this guy isn't doing you any favors in attracting potential suitors. He'd make a great bodyguard if you were some big celebrity, but I pity the poor soul trying to move in and sweep you off your feet."

"Potential suitors?" Sarah mocked.

Emmie smiled. "What are you saying, Finn? I never knew you

had such strong feelings for me." She stepped closer to him and ran her fingers down his chest.

Sarah folded her arms over her chest and glared at him.

Finn smirked and gently removed Emmie's hand while glancing back at John nervously. "Yeah... not referring to me..."

"You've romanced a ghost, but you're scared of John?" Sarah prodded.

"Well, not really *scared*. I'm sure he's really charming somewhere deep, *deep* beneath that icy stare and permanent scowl, but the man's got no boundaries." He lowered his voice and inched toward Emmie. "If you don't stand up for yourself with this guy, he'll be right there to chaperone every date after demanding a blood sample and a background test."

Emmie laughed. "John wouldn't go *that* far. Maybe a police escort to and from the movie."

Sarah added to the laughter.

John looked over, then finished his call and turned to them. "They're on their way."

Finn cleared his throat and avoided eye contact with John as he stepped into their circle and stood with his arms folded across his chest.

John was grinning now. A mischievous grin as if someone had just shared a nasty joke. Maybe someone had, on the phone, but he glanced side-eyed at Finn even as Emmie shifted the conversation away from the woman in the basement.

"Read any good books lately, John?" Emmie asked him.

John didn't take his eyes off Finn. "Plenty. Always reading, always learning, always trying to figure people out."

A silence passed between them until John chuckled, then threw his arm over Finn's shoulders. "Maybe I was wrong about you."

Finn met John's stare with a puzzled expression. "Oh?"

"You're okay."

"I am?" Finn leaned away.

"Sure. When I first met you, messing around in the cemetery

over the summer, I thought you were just one of *them*. One of those wacky ghost hunters. But, you know, nobody would have found that poor woman here in the basement unless you'd been putzing around with stuff you shouldn't have been putzing with."

Finn nodded slowly. "That's true."

"And you've been helping Emmie a lot lately, especially with that old woman's house next to yours in Lake Eden, haven't you?"

"I try my best."

"Sure, you do. You've earned your right to hang around with these two gals."

Finn paused and his eyes widened. "Thank you?"

John laughed. "Definitely wrong about you." He walked into the kitchen and filled a glass with water before returning a minute later. "You'd make a mighty fine suitor to either one of these young ladies."

Finn slumped forward and covered his face for a moment before looking at John with deep remorse. "You heard me?"

"I might be a little older, a little wiser, and a little scarier, but my hearing is top notch."

"Sorry, John..." Emmie said.

John held up his hand. "No need to apologize for anything. Everything he said is right. I think our acquaintanceship just moved to the next level. Good to hear him standing up for you. I can't be there for you all the time, Emmie, so I feel better knowing a guy like Finn has your back."

Emmie laughed. "You okay, Finn?" He moved back and leaned against the corner of the couch. "You need a drink?"

"Yes, please."

Emmie passed out a round of beers—John even accepted one —and they drank until the investigators showed up thirty minutes later.

Two men arrived from the coroner's office first, with another two officers arriving a short time later with a long list of questions. But John was right there to guide them through any awkwardness, such as how the body had been discovered and Emmie's past history of leading police to Frankie's body at the lake.

But within fifteen minutes, they were free to go. John suggested it might take a couple of hours to remove the body, so Emmie told him they were headed out.

"Don't blame you," John said. "I'll lock up if you're not back when we're done."

Emmie nodded and gestured for Finn and Sarah to follow her as she grabbed her laptop from the living room and headed to the front door.

Finn stepped outside first, with Emmie and Sarah right behind him. John followed them to the doorway as they headed toward Emmie's Toyota Corolla.

"A bodyguard?" John chuckled.

Finn turned back and cringed. "Maybe not the best analogy."

Arriving at the car, Sarah asked, "Where are we headed?"

"Somewhere we can talk in private. We can't wait for the investigators to tell us who that woman is, *if* they ever bother to find out." Emmie climbed into the driver's seat of her car, and Sarah sat in the passenger seat, with Finn in the back. After the doors closed, she tapped her laptop. "I've got a million questions, so I think it's best if we all focus on getting answers."

Emmie looked back at John. He was talking on his phone again. Her gaze jumped to the upstairs bedroom window. Alice's silhouette shifted within the shadows.

8

Emmie located an empty table in the farthest corner of The Sunshine Café and set up her laptop. Finn and Sarah sat next to her as she scrolled through pages of Internet searches that resulted in vague information about the early history of Green Hills. After only a few minutes, Emmie let out an exasperated sigh. "How would I find info on that woman?"

"There's got to be something about her online," Sarah said. "Maybe a missing person report from long ago?"

"Who could we ask to find out her identity, besides the authorities?" Emmie looked at Finn. "Would it help to visit City Hall? I'm sure they've got records for all the details about my house. We could find the names of the previous owners and see if any Hyde family descendents are still in the area. Maybe a relative of Daniel and Ruth would know a little info about them, or at least it would give us a place to start. I'm pretty sure I remember my parents mentioning that they built the house right around the time when Alice killed herself, so I'm assuming they did some research on her."

"You won't find public property records like that for free on the Internet," Finn said. "I've tried before, and it's private. Like you said, normally we'd need to go to City Hall, since that's where all the property records for the county are stored. But I've done similar research on haunted houses through the county using their paid account to grab all that kind of info. It should show us all the background details on the stuff we need. I'll see if I can dig up something. Mind if I borrow your laptop?"

Emmie pushed it in front of him, and within seconds his fingers clattered over the keyboard.

A couple of minutes later, his eyes widened after stopping on a webpage. Emmie and Sarah leaned in beside him.

"Daniel and Ruth Hyde owned your house until 1922," Finn said.

Emmie nodded. "That sounds right. And Alice hung herself in 1921, so about a year before they moved. My parents bought it in 1999 when I was about three, if I remember correctly."

Finn pointed to the screen. "Here they are, all the owners right up to present day. Ed and Shannon Fisher purchased it in 1999 for the amazingly low price of $107,000. They got a great deal."

"Because it was haunted," Emmie added. "No one had lived there in a while. Everyone who bought it moved away and then took a while to sell it."

"Would it help if we talked to any of the previous owners?" Sarah asked, then answered herself, "Though I guess finding the owners close to the time of the Hyde family would be tricky, as they would be dead?"

"Easier to just find any living Hydes." Finn made a search that led to a different webpage and revealed a long list of people named Hyde. "There's a few dozen around the Minneapolis area and more in the surrounding counties. The trick is finding out where Daniel and Ruth Hyde moved to after leaving this house, and *why* they left here."

"If the body in the basement is Ruth," Emmie asked, "do you think Daniel could have killed her before moving out, and then left her buried in the old house? Knowing he was selling it?"

"I wonder if renovations were that common back then?" Finn asked.

Emmie considered the question. "I think not. Not the craze it is now, when people just tear everything down to make bigger rooms or suites with bathrooms."

"So," Sarah said, "burying someone behind a wall might have been a pretty safe way of hiding a body and a crime."

"More than a few bodies have been found like that." Finn's face brightened. "And gold. Less often."

"Even if it's not Ruth down there, someone was obviously murdered," Emmie said, "and it could have been around the time Alice died, judging by the clothes and the fact they left then."

"Before jumping to conclusions, we should gather more facts," Finn said. "No sense in speculating at this point."

"What should we do now?"

Finn chuckled. "Digging up people is my specialty."

"That's a little awkward." Sarah nudged him.

He rolled his eyes and went on, "I've got some tricks up my sleeve. Just give me a few minutes." Finn searched through several more web pages, then scrolled down over a page referencing someone named Hyde in Summerton, Minnesota. Clicking on a couple more links, he came to a list of obituaries. They were digital scans of old newspapers, but the highlighted text stopped on one of them. "Here we go. Daniel's obituary."

There passed away at Summerton on July 2ND, 1934, at the home of the Hyde family, a young and respected resident in the person of Daniel Hyde, aged 38 years, beloved husband of Ruth Hyde, who is left to mourn; also one daughter Grace Hyde at home. Daniel's passing follows his younger sister Alice by thirteen years, and the passing of their parents by fifteen years. May his soul Rest In Peace.

～

"SUMMERTON." EMMIE'S EYES LIT UP. "THAT'S NOT TOO FAR away."

"That narrows it down a bit, but it also rules out that the body downstairs is Ruth Hyde. Unless he killed her and passed off someone else for his wife." Finn threw Sarah a look. "Men are so evil they do that, you know."

Finn searched again using the city parameters. "If they purchased their new home in Summerton, then Grace Hyde or her relatives might still live in the area. Though if she is still alive, she might be in her mid-nineties."

"She could totally be alive," Sarah said. "The old people at the hospital keep saying someone died 'very young' if they were in their early eighties."

"I guess a hundred is the new eighty. Just give me a minute." Finn went to a separate address search account that must have been for his journalistic job and stopped on a list of names. "There *are* a few Hyde family names in Summerton."

Finn went silent again and scoured through more web pages. A minute later, he pointed at the computer screen.

"One house was built in 1922, the same year Daniel and Ruth moved there. That's got to be it." Finn took his phone and photographed the address.

"So we'll just knock on their door and ask about Daniel Hyde right off the bat?" Sarah asked. "Shouldn't we have a better reason for showing up?"

Emmie thought about it. "I could mention something I found here in my house, maybe some of the old stuff I found in the attic. There isn't much. And Alice's music box? I could take it with us."

"Won't Alice have a problem with that?"

"I'll bring it back."

At another search, Finn brought up a black-and-white photo of an old country two-story home. "I found a photo of the place.

Daniel and Ruth's home in Summerton. Might look different now, since the city has grown a lot."

Emmie stared at it. The photo didn't show much, but the style of Hyde House was similar to her own house, although it was larger and a little more ornate around the edges. "Even if it's the wrong person, they might know where to find the Hydes. It's the best chance we have."

However, Finn was still clicking through several windows and stopped on a small piece of text.

"Well, what do you know?" He grinned, while leaning back and crossing his arms. "The current owner is listed as Grace Hyde."

※ 9 ※

Someone had left on all the lights.

Arriving back at Hanging House later that evening, Emmie stared up at the bedroom window where she'd seen the figure of Alice earlier, but no one was there now.

"Either Alice is furious about all the unwanted guests in her house, or John forgot to turn off the lights."

"Maybe both," Sarah said.

"Well... goodnight, gals." After a wary glance at the window, Finn gave each of them a hug and gestured to his car. "Time for some sweet dreams before we continue this adventure tomorrow. You'll pick me up at ten?"

"We'll be there."

After Finn left, Emmie and Sarah walked inside the house. Nothing was out of place in the living room or kitchen, although that wasn't much of a surprise since the investigator and electrician had done their work in the basement.

John had used his key to lock up and left a note hanging in the doorway to the kitchen, apologizing for the mess in the basement and informing her about the paperwork on the counter that she would need to fill out as soon as possible. He offered to help seal up the hole from which the coroners had removed the woman and recommended that Emmie not do anymore digging without a licensed electrician. But, he noted cheerfully, she had electricity again after he'd temporarily wired things back up again.

But even though the lights in Sarah's apartment were on, Emmie still didn't think John had done that.

"Something's up with Alice," she said. "I hope John didn't have any trouble with her while taking care of everything."

Sarah gestured to John's note. "He didn't say anything about ghosts."

"I'm not sure he'd admit it even if he did see something."

Emmie walked through the kitchen with Sarah and peered into the basement. The lights were on down there too.

"At least they're working," Sarah said.

"I'll take care of it. See you in the morning."

"All right." Emmie descended the stairs alone.

Just like on the main floor, every light in the basement was on and all the doors were open, including the bathroom at the bottom of the stairs where Frankie had died. Bits of dirt and dust were scattered over the basement floor. Remnants of the corpse they'd removed?

The mess Finn had made still covered the floor in the room where the corpse was found. Someone had swept the bricks and debris to the side, most likely to clear a path and remove the woman, but the gaping hole was empty. The wires were patched up, just like John had mentioned in his note. No more flickering lights, at least until Alice's next tantrum.

There was still work to be done, but she had no energy to take care of anything else that day, so she switched off the lights and headed back to her room, wondering if she might see Alice again before going to sleep.

Emmie played the musical box next to her bed, just like she always did, but Alice didn't appear for the first time since Emmie had agreed to play it. It would take a while to smooth things out again.

Oh, shit. I really upset her.

And she had forgotten to ask Sarah if she had any strong feelings within the house. That might have revealed how Alice was reacting to their earlier conversation, but there wasn't much she could do about it now—she could barely keep her eyes open. Everything would need to wait until morning.

She prepared for bed and climbed under the covers, and within minutes she was hovering at the edge of sleep. Darkness clouded her mind, but the murky face of an old woman hung in her imagination.

Grace Hyde's face; an elderly version of Alice if she had lived a full life, wrinkled and weathered. She smiled and reached out, beckoning Emmie to come inside a house.

It wasn't a difficult decision. The smell of freshly baked bread and the sight of radiant rays of sunshine beaming through the open windows cheered Emmie's heart.

Grace wasn't like Alice at all. Hard to believe they were related. No cries of an adolescent girl's furious assertion—"*My house!*" This woman offered it as, "*Your house. Emmie's house.*"

And Emmie didn't hesitate before stepping inside.

The sound of a girl's laughter snapped her back to reality.

She recognized Alice's voice again—the same laughter she had heard when John had been there—but the girl was talking to someone as if engaged in a conversation. Conversation with whom? The recipient of her words didn't answer, so it couldn't be Sarah.

Fragments of their conversation hung in the air.

"... take me..."

"... so different from... Daniel coming back?"

"... long time..."

Emmie climbed out of bed and followed Alice's voice, stopping at the small door leading into the attic. The light from the attic streamed out from beneath the door as she stood quietly and listened to Alice's laughter. It was comforting to hear the girl's cheerful voice, but it was so strange not being able to hear the other person with her.

Turning the handle slowly to keep Alice from running away, she opened the door and flipped on the light.

Inside, a woman was sitting on the floor across from Alice, facing away. It was the woman from the basement, judging by her hair and clothing, but she was finely dressed now, her hair straight and clean—a stark contrast to her corpse.

They were playing with a discarded white marble, no doubt left over from Frankie's collection, rolling it across the floor to each other with great difficulty. When it reached one of them, she laughed as if scoring some glorious victory. Emmie hesitated to bother them, fearing Alice might disappear again, but she wanted to get a better look at the woman they had found inside the wall.

"Alice?" Emmie asked with a smile.

Alice didn't respond.

Emmie cleared her throat. "Who's your friend?"

Alice stopped laughing, but she didn't lose her smile.

"I heard someone talking in here," Emmie said. "It's nice to see you having fun."

The woman remained seated but craned her neck around and stared at Emmie.

Her mouth was sewn shut.

The woman strained to open her mouth as if the stitches were nothing more than a nuisance, and it was obvious she had a lot to say. Her jaw opened and closed as she tried to express herself, and her lips stretched, straining the limits of the stitches, but not a sound escaped her throat. Her eyes were a beautiful brown, and somewhere within that sorrowful stare the woman pleaded for relief, but there was nothing Emmie could do about her voice.

Footsteps came from the hallway. Emmie was unwittingly backing away and bumped into Sarah, who came up behind her. "What's the matter?"

"Do you see her?" Emmie asked.

"I see Alice's form, and I think there's someone next to her."

"It's the woman from the basement."

Sarah gasped while taking Emmie's hand and squeezing.

"She doesn't live in the basement," Alice said. "She lives downstairs." Alice turned to Sarah. "Next to your room, where that other woman lived for a while, the one who killed the boy."

"Is she your friend?" Emmie asked.

"She's my nanny. Catherine came back. I knew she would come back, eventually."

"The woman's lips are sewn together," Emmie whispered to her friend and moved closer to Alice, letting go of Sarah. "Alice, can you tell us what happened to Catherine?"

"She went on a trip, but she's back."

"I mean, why did we find her in the basement? Did someone hurt her?"

Alice glanced at Catherine, then laughed. "What do you mean? She's not hurt. We're playing."

"I see that, but something bad happened to her. Can she tell us? Do you know what happened?"

Emmie moved around into the attic and faced the woman, with Sarah moving beside her. Looking directly into Catherine's eyes, Emmie asked her, "Who did this to you?"

No response from the woman. No surprise since her mouth was sewn shut, but this time she didn't even try to speak.

"Did someone murder you?" Sarah insisted.

"That's ridiculous." Alice laughed. "Don't you see her? She's right there in front of you. She's not dead."

Emmie looked up and down at the woman's spirit form, searching for any clues that might give away a cause of death. No visible signs of trauma, except for the sewn mouth. It must have been poison, then.

Alice stepped in front of them and pulled Catherine away. "She doesn't want to talk right now. She's shy. And we're playing, so go away."

Sarah nudged Emmie, then whispered something in her ear. "Em, something is odd about this spirit."

Emmie and Sarah stepped away, then looked over their shoulders back at Alice and the woman. "Like what?"

"I don't feel any emotions from her. Everyone has an aura of emotions emanating from them, at least a little—even Alice—but something is gone from this woman. Almost like her spirit is dead, if that's possible."

"Well, that's a new one."

"Let me try something." Sarah stepped forward and offered

her hand in the general direction of the woman. "May I touch you?"

Alice jumped in. "Do it, Catherine; it's really wonderful, what Sarah can do."

Emmie watched the woman hold out her hand slowly, and Sarah touched her along the back of her wrist. A moment after they touched, Sarah yanked back and gasped. "Oh, my God."

"What?"

Sarah shuddered. "She's frozen inside, like a block of ice."

Nothing in Catherine's physical appearance suggested anything was different from any other spirit she'd seen, except for her mouth. "Her physical mouth wasn't sewn shut, was it?"

"No. But... the doll."

"Time's up," Alice said, moving away with Catherine. "We want to play alone again. I haven't seen Catherine in such a long time."

"Yes." Emmie nodded and stepped back.

Alice moved to the far side of the attic with her nanny, and they began playing with the marble again.

"We can't release Catherine now," Sarah said. "Alice would never talk to us again if we separated her from that joy. And the woman obviously has unfinished business here. Something's very wrong."

"I'm too tired, anyway." Emmie sighed. "I guess we have another guest in the house."

"Catherine's not a guest," Alice said sternly, making them jump. "She lives here. *You're* the guest."

"Of course," Emmie said. "Sarah and I just wanted to make sure you're okay. We'll go to bed now. But first, Alice, let me ask you a question. Would you mind if I borrowed your music box tomorrow? I promise I'll bring it back to play your song at night."

"I don't like anyone taking my things."

Emmie swallowed. "I won't take it, just borrow it so I can listen to it, and I'll bring it back tomorrow night, I promise."

Alice waited a few seconds before answering. "If you don't bring it back, I won't let you sleep... I also promise."

E mmie glanced into the rearview mirror on their way to
       Hyde House. Finn was in the backseat working on his
laptop again. "What are you doing back there?"

Finn looked up half-dazedly at her until his eyes focused on
the rearview mirror and he smiled. "Research. Thing is, our
whole lives seem to lead back to New Orleans." He held up a
hand. "Spare me the mention of you-know-who. What I mean is
that voodoo is sort of an umbrella term for magic."

"I read that," Emmie said.

He ignored her. "Meaning that it's a hybrid of African and
Christian mythology with Caribbean belief systems. Voodoo is
Haiti when you call it like that, but it's a catch-all name for when
different religions or schools of thought merge. In America, it
started in New Orleans also because of the African influence."

"And Josephine brought it here," Emmie concluded.

He blew out a breath. "People like her. Witches like her, yes.
And then in the Midwest it got mixed with farming and Puri-
tanism. So good luck to us."

Sarah raised her eyebrows at Emmie. "We are three Puritan
descendants. Good luck to us is right."

They kept talking up a storm along the way to Summerton

about magic and different beliefs, and how in the end it was all so similar—but as they approached the town, they fell quiet.

Emmie glanced over at the box of gifts sitting in Sarah's lap. They had scoured the attic in the early hours, looking through whatever was there to see if they could find things no one had ever bothered to throw out. Lucky, perhaps, that the successive owners of Hanging House had never stayed long and had most likely abandoned some things in the attic in the rush to leave.

An oversized ceramic mug lay on its side inside the box and she spotted the initials pressed into the bottom. RLM. *Ruth... L?... M?...* The initials might be enough to get Alice's niece talking, if she were lively enough to receive them and accepted their excuse for stopping by.

She practiced what she would say when Grace came to the door. *These are from your Aunt Alice's house.* Aunt Alice. It was so strange to think that Alice would have been someone's aunt if she hadn't killed herself. Maybe she would have had children of her own, and grandkids. She had cut off an entire family tree with one dark act.

Or had her brother done that?

Arriving at the edge of Summerton, Emmie turned off onto a side road and reminded herself that the visit wasn't only about solving the murder of Alice's nanny, Catherine, although that was very much on their mind. The deeper reason was that Alice needed—deserved—peace. Emmie had promised herself to free Alice someday, and the girl's longing for her brother to return home pointed a way to do that. If Alice was ever going to find peace, Emmie and Sarah would need to step up and make it happen. And Finn, who kept looking at his computer and not saying anything.

When they finally pulled into its driveway, Hyde House was just as she had pictured it in her mind after seeing the black-and-white photo earlier. An old white house with Victorian-style designs built along the edges. Larger than Emmie's house, maybe twice the size, but nothing too extravagant.

Emmie parked the car, and they stepped out into the cool mid-morning air. Finn was the last to emerge, snapping his laptop shut and leaving it in the backseat.

Holding the box of gifts against her chest, Emmie led them up the sidewalk to the front door. The contents were visible to whoever might peek out the window and see strangers approaching, so they wouldn't think they were religious solicitors, at least.

"I hope this goes well," Sarah said.

"Who can resist that smile?" Finn said.

The door opened and a woman about sixty years old answered it.

"Hello?" She scowled at them, cracking the door open only a few inches. Her eyes narrowed at the box of gifts.

"Hi, my name is Emmie, and I'm sorry to bother you, but is this the home of Grace Hyde?"

The woman paused, glancing from one to the other. "Yes. We don't want to buy anything." She scowled. "And we won't contribute to charities. We have our own."

Emmie widened her smile. "We're not selling anything. I'm Emmie Fisher, and I live in Hang—" She paused. "... in the house where her parents used to live in Green Hills. I was just cleaning out the attic and found some items that might have belonged to them. At least, they do seem to be from that time, and have initials on them. We thought she might like to get them back."

Still looking unfriendly, and angrier, if anything, the woman shook her head again but opened the door a little further, revealing a husky body hunched forward and draped in a dull green dress. Her hair was dyed a harsh dark color. "She doesn't need anything like that."

Another dark-haired woman, half the first one's age, had been listening to the exchange and came to the door, pushing it wider and greeting them with a bright smile. Her pink and white outfit was a trendy style, and she stood tall with an elegant, confident stare.

"You can't just decide for Grandma, Mom!" she exclaimed, eyeing the box of gifts.

Emmie moved into the doorway, holding on to the box, as she wanted them to be invited in and not be forced to hand it over. "I think these items belonged to Ruth Hyde. I own the house now, and when I discovered Grace was still alive, I thought she might get a kick out of having them."

"We won't pay for anything," the older woman said sharply.

The young woman nudged her aside. "Well, this is a wonderful surprise. I know my grandma will love to have them." She motioned them in, offering her hand to each.

As they had already gained entrance to the house, Finn took the box from Emmie, and their young hostess went on. "I'm Veronica, by the way. That's my mom, Zelda. Don't mind her at all. She gets a bit cranky when strangers come to the door. Please come in." Veronica gestured for them to follow her, and Zelda went on ahead without waiting.

The air inside the house was almost as cold as outside, but they could see through large doors to the left that there was a muted fire in the living room fireplace. A pleasant burnt-wood smell filled the hall. The walls were covered in outdated wallpaper and sprawling rugs lay over the wood floors that squeaked under their feet. Several antique framed paintings adorned the walls, but there were many contemporary ones as well. Mixed in with the paintings on the hall were a few scattered framed photos, although they featured landscapes and buildings and not people.

The living room had a light-brown leather couch and its matching loveseat beside a weathered armchair. Sitting on a side table next to the recliner was a small gold bell and eyeglasses next to a few hardcover books. A vase full of flowers sat atop another side table, and an oak coffee table in the middle of everything displayed a green and white floral arrangement centered over a white lace runner. Two bookcases sat side-by-side against one wall, with all the shelves filled with hardcovers, probably untouched for years judging by the carefully placed, colorful knickknacks decorating the space in front of them. A sprawling chandelier hung overhead, but sunlight brightened the room, streaming in between violet curtains through the room's two large windows. But the centerpiece in the room was a massive stone fireplace with a thick mantelpiece lined with decorative potted plants, framed photos of Veronica, and antique candlestick holders, one on each end.

Another smell hung in the air. Not an unpleasant smell, but a somewhat odd and distinct scent of cleaning products and old wood. Emmie stepped in further.

"Did we come at a bad time?" Emmie asked.

"Not at all." Veronica turned to her mother. "Let's get Grandma. She's going to love this."

Zelda grumbled while stepping aside as Veronica motioned for them to sit. Even before they did, she peered into the box of gifts and pulled out a small painting in an ornate picture frame. It showed a farmhouse and rolling hills behind it, an impression of what the land around Green Hills must have looked like in the early 1900s.

"This is interesting," Veronica said, looking like she thought the opposite. She didn't wait for Emmie to respond before picking up the ceramic mug and pretending that it weighed a hundred pounds. "Imagine having to lift this thing to drink your coffee."

Emmie opened her mouth to say something, but a noise came from a doorway across the room and a moment later a frail old lady stepped in with the help of a tall, brunette woman in khaki scrubs who could only have been a nurse.

The old woman's eyes lit up when she saw them. "Look at this, we have guests!" She clung to the nurse's arm, even as Zelda stepped over and held the old woman's other arm.

Grace.

Emmie thought that for someone almost a century old, she truly didn't look a day over eighty. Her elegant white dress hid most of her thin frame, and her hair was cut short, yet styled with care as if they'd caught her on her way to church.

"Grandma," Veronica said while still inspecting the items in the box, "come over here, look what they brought us."

"What is it?" Grace asked, shuffling forward.

"They live in your parents' old house back in that small city," Veronica said. "They found some things that might have belonged to them and were kind enough to bring them over."

Grace's face formed a curious expression. "Oh? Let's have a look."

Zelda and the nurse steadied Grace before easing her into the recliner. As her body sank into the chair's cloth cushions, a couple of her joints popped, although she seemed not to notice. After checking with Grace, the nurse stepped back. Now Zelda stood against the wall, watching from a distance with her arms folded over her chest.

Veronica lifted the mug of the box and placed it in Grace's lap. "Here's the first one, Grandma."

"Would you look at this!" Grace struggled to lift it, yet turned it over in her hands as her eyes welled up with tears, then ran her fingertips over the letters. "Oh, my mother's initials. *RLM.* Her maiden name was McDougall, though she was always so proud of being Mrs. Hyde. It must have belonged to her before they'd gotten married." She pulled out a maroon fringed silk scarf. A tear streamed down her cheek. "And this must have been my father's scarf. It's in such good shape, after all this time. Look, she must have embroidered his initials. So in love until their last day." She held the item up and sniffed it, then smiled. "Doesn't smell like him anymore. He had the most wonderful smell of Lifebuoy Soap, although I'm sure they don't make it anymore." Grace turned in her seat with some difficulty and faced Zelda. "Have you offered our guests coffee?"

Zelda straightened and looked down before shaking her head. "Not yet."

"You must have some coffee with us," Grace said to the guests.

Emmie nodded with thanks; not that they needed coffee, but it would allow them to stay longer.

Grace stared at Zelda until she walked off toward the kitchen.

"This is Donna," Grace said, motioning to the nurse. "She keeps me on my toes. Well, on my feet, most days."

Sarah exclaimed, "I'm also a nurse."

Donna's hair was frazzled and her eyes were tired, but she lit up at hearing Sarah's words. "Do you also work in home healthcare?"

"No, at a hospital in Minneapolis."

"I'm only an LPN." Donna shrugged. "Maybe someday."

"Let's see those dry hands!" On the sofa, Veronica scooted closer to her grandmother's chair and grasped her fingers while taking a white bottle of lotion from the side table. She began rubbing one of Grace's hands as the old woman motioned for Donna to take the box with the antiques and place it on a chair nearby.

Veronica said, "I've got my own private line of skin creams. That's what I do for a living."

"What sort of creams?" Sarah asked.

"Organic mixes I've created myself. This one does wonders for Grandma's eczema." Veronica stood, rubbing the excess cream into her own hands, then pulled a business card from a small pink purse and handed it to Emmie. "Call me, or stop by my store before you leave today. I'd love to give you a treat for being so kind. Downtown Summerton."

Emmie nodded while examining it, then put it into her pocket.

Zelda returned a short time later carrying four cups of coffee, a jar of coffee creamer, and a flowery sugar bowl balanced on a silver tray. She laid the tray on the table and handed out each coffee without expression, adding sugar and cream as requested.

"Thank you." Emmie nodded to Zelda and Grace, although Grace was staring up at her daughter with tired and somewhat displeased eyes.

Finn took his eyes off Veronica long enough to glance over at Emmie. The subtle gesture with his head toward their gifts reminded her that it was best to keep the conversation focused on their visit's primary purpose: obtaining answers. She leaned over toward the box that no longer held Grace's attention and lifted out Alice's music box. "And this?"

Grace set down her coffee with a perplexed look. "I'm not sure what that is."

"It's pretty," Veronica said, taking it. She opened it, and the music started playing, but it made her grandmother wrinkle her nose and frown. Veronica laughed. "Oh, she doesn't like this one."

Emmie accepted it back and almost sighed with relief. That would avert any issues with Alice. "I'm thinking it might have belonged to your Aunt Alice."

Grace shrugged and steadied her coffee as her hands trembled. "Possibly."

"Did your mom talk much about your father's younger sister?" Sarah asked.

Grace's eyes glazed over. "A little." The cup slipped from her hand and smashed against the wooden floors. Glass shards scattered in every direction. "Oh, dear!"

Zelda lost no time lashing out at Veronica. "See, I told you the hand cream is too oily."

"It's perfect," Grace protested. She turned to Veronica. "I want you to bring me more. Smells so good, too."

"Donna," Zelda said, averting her eyes, as if keeping her mother from commanding her to clean up the mess.

Finn stood and rounded up the shards with the side of his shoe as the nurse slowly left to the kitchen.

"Leave it, young man," Grace told him.

Within a few minutes, Donna had come with a broom, duster and mop and cleaned up the spilled coffee and the shards.

Grace laughed. "I'm sorry," she said to them. "Zelda is too hard on the girl."

"Too hard on her?" Zelda scoffed.

Grace rolled her eyes and chuckled. "Where were we?" the old woman asked.

"Your aunt?" Finn offered a handsome smile that did not fail to soothe the old woman. He stood by her chair, leaning against the side of the mantelpiece, and she began speaking directly to him.

"I know it was a terrible death. She was a sick girl, I heard. Very sick. And it's so terrible for a child to hang herself..." Her eyes teared up again. "My father couldn't bear it, how his sister had died, and I believe it contributed to his death at thirty-eight..." She paused and wiped her eyes. "He killed himself too, you know."

Finn's gaze shifted toward Emmie, but jumped back to Grace. It was obvious he wanted to look over at his friends, but the three Hyde women were watching him and he kept his face neutral as Sarah took a nervous sip of her coffee while Emmie waited with bated breath for the rest of the story.

"He never recovered fully after Alice died," Grace went on. "Never the same after that, according to what Mom told me. It's impossibly hard to go on after someone you love dies like that. He felt guilty, you see."

Emmie nodded slowly, still holding back her shock at the news that Alice's brother had also committed suicide—and Grace's suggestion that it had possibly happened because of Alice's hanging. Her heart ached as she tried to understand why Alice would have killed herself in the first place; it was impossible to find out unless the girl also accepted the truth of what she had done.

"That's so awful," Sarah said.

Another tear dripped down Grace's cheek. "Selfish girl, to do that. My mother said she needed a lot of attention, and my father believed he had not given her enough. He had never harmed a fly in his life and apparently doted on his sister. Mom never got over the shock of finding him."

The sadness of the situation clouded Emmie's mind, but a new possibility emerged. If Daniel had killed himself in the house, he might still be there. To find out, she would need to move off to a room alone soon and try to contact him.

She looked over at Sarah and their eyes met. *She's thinking the same thing.*

Veronica leaned forward and wiped the tears off her grandmother's face. Grace smiled and patted her hand. "At least I still have the comfort of knowing they are together forever in the backyard. Their graves sit side by side, just like she wanted."

"That's beautiful," Sarah said.

"It is, isn't it? I put in a flower garden around the graves to remind myself of the love they shared." She gestured to the box of gifts. "You know, Daniel's parents built the house where you found this just for Alice, so she would always have a place to live. And she went and hung herself there instead."

"So after Alice died," Finn jumped in, "your family sold the house and moved here?"

"That's right. I was born here."

Veronica reached into the box again and pulled out the last item, an ornate silver plate that must have been lying against the bottom. She handed it to Grace, who read the inscription: "*Mr. and Mrs. Daniel Hyde, June 16th, 1919.* This was from their wedding day. I miss my mother so much. You know, she died in a fire at our family business. It devastated me. Thankfully, she died quickly. The flames didn't get her, but the smoke inhalation did. I lost so much, but at least I had my little Zelda to keep me company." Her glance at her less-than-charming daughter held some humor. "And then Zelda found love, had my lovely Veronica, divorced the poor man, and we've been here ever since."

"Three helpless women," Veronica said sarcastically, then

checked her watch and stood. "Business calls. Got to go, I'm afraid."

"That's my girl," Grace said. "Always focused on life."

They said goodbye to Veronica before she headed out the door. Silence filled the room for several seconds, until Finn looked around and said, "The other grandchildren must find it interesting to visit your house. So much history here."

"No other grandchildren than what you see. All the Hyde family members are either deceased or divorced." Grace chuckled. "The future of the family seems to lie with Veronica now."

Zelda grunted. "If she's the hope for the family, then we're all doomed."

Grace glared at Zelda. "Always so jealous."

That bickering could not go on in front of guests for long, and the old lady would tire soon. Emmie would need to act fast if she planned to communicate with Daniel. She scanned the shelves and walls for a picture of him. "Would you happen to have a photo of your parents? It'd be interesting to see what the people who lived in my house looked like."

Grace nodded. "Yes, dear, you should see a photo of them on the wall down that hallway." She pointed back toward the stairway going upstairs. "Feel free to have a look."

Emmie stood. "Is the bathroom back there also?"

"Oh I'm sorry, I should have offered." Grace turned to Zelda. "Show her to the bathroom. Or is that too much for you?"

Without replying, Zelda led Emmie down the hall.

It led straight out to a porch, but several closed doors lay between the stairway going upstairs and the yard. The hallway veered off to the side just before the exit. From the front, the house hadn't appeared so large, but now Emmie realized there were many more rooms at the back.

On her way, she paused at a framed black and white portrait on the wall showing a young man and woman and a new baby as they stood beside the door to Hyde House. *Daniel, Ruth, and Grace.*

Zelda slowed but did not turn back. "That's the bathroom door up ahead."

Emmie studied Daniel's face. He had the same features as Alice, although he had short hair and a friendly face. But there was one trait Alice and Daniel shared: an intense stare.

Daniel, let's talk.

At the bathroom door a little further along, Zelda left her. As soon as Emmie closed the door, she shut her eyes and meditated, picturing Daniel's face in her mind.

Good, now I can see you.

Opening herself to any sensations of a spirit nearby, Emmie pulled from the darkness. If Daniel really killed himself in the house, she would see him soon. She strained for a few minutes, curling her fingers into fists.

Where are you, Daniel?

Spirits lurked out there, far beyond the house, lost souls drawn by her beacon of concentration. She felt them moving toward her, but she didn't recognize any of them as Daniel.

Still, there was something within the energy connecting her to him. A thin, vague stream of his *essence* nearby. She could see his face so clearly, but still she couldn't draw him closer.

Come on, Daniel, we need to get some answers.

It was taking too long. She couldn't be in the bathroom much longer without arousing suspicion. She focused on Daniel's eyes, staring into the mental image, and screamed into his soul.

Where are you?

His image shifted in her mind. His eyes had come alive for a moment, stared back at her, but then faded away again before she could reach out to him. He slipped away, and it was too late.

N one of them spoke until they sat in the car again with the doors closed.

"Any luck?" Finn asked.

Emmie started the car. "Nothing. I got the sense that Daniel's around—somewhere—but I couldn't connect with him. I'm not sure why I had so much trouble. It's possible that since he committed suicide, he might not want to be seen."

Sarah frowned. "I guess that means no more information about Catherine either."

"We're back to square one," Finn said. "Though there must be something or someone we can pull from." The silence went on deceptively long before he said, "What about that, uh, what's-her-name... oh, Veronica."

The two women exchanged a glance and shook their heads at the same time.

"If you remembered to learn a love spell, Finn," Sarah shot over her shoulder with a sneer, "she might tell us secrets."

In the rearview mirror, Emmie watched Finn's eyes open wide. Should she tell him that was a huge tell? Always happened when he was feigning innocence.

"What do you mean?" Finn asked.

Emmie scoffed. "Seriously? You think we didn't see that?"

"Boy, could you have stared at her legs any more than you did?" Sarah rolled her eyes.

"Jealous?" Finn asked with a smile.

"Pretty rude," Sarah mumbled.

"You know what was rude?" Finn asked. "The mother and Zelda."

Emmie smirked. Finn obviously wanted them to forget about it. "Okay, it's not important. Let's drive out of here first." She gently shook her head while backing out of the driveway as if the women inside might be able to hear them.

Sarah didn't wait long to talk about the palpable awkwardness in the house. "I don't know whether to feel sorry for Zelda or that she might deserve it."

"Longlegs and the old lady are no easy roommates, I bet," Emmie said as she drove. "Two women to reckon with."

"Who would marry Zelda?" Finn asked in a small voice, as if he were really trying to picture someone.

Sarah nodded. "I know... A poor man indeed!"

"Should we go see Veronica?" Emmie asked. "She might share more details away from her family."

"Nothing to lose," Finn said, staring out the window.

Emmie rummaged through her pocket for the business card. "Didn't seem like she knew or cared about the past, but she was friendly, at least. And you know, the discovery of Catherine's body will probably be in the newspapers tomorrow."

"We could fess up," Sarah said. "Gain her trust."

They all agreed it was a good plan; or a plan, at least. Emmie followed her GPS across town, and turned left into a small outdoor retail mall. It was in a newer, nicer area of town, and they found Veronica's business without any trouble. The large glass windows lit a bright, clean interior. Skincare displays and glamorous photos of models with perfect skin filled the walls, and unseen sources of ambient light came from every direction as they moved to the empty front desk.

A moment later, Veronica stepped out from the back room with a surprised but bright grin on her face. "Oh, it's wonderful to see you again."

"We wanted to talk with you about some other things we didn't mention at your house," Sarah said.

Veronica tilted her head. "Oh? What's that?"

"It's that—" Emmie started. "We didn't want to bother you with it, but the things we gave your grandmother weren't the only things we found in the Green Hills house. There was something else we found in the basement. It kind of... shocked us."

Veronica leaned in with a curious smile. "I imagine it wasn't money or jewelry?"

"Not exactly. We found... the body of a young woman buried behind a brick wall."

Now Veronica's eyes widened. "That *is* quite a surprise." She looked from one to the other, and then at Finn, who had stayed by the displays. "I see. And you didn't mention it before because—"

"We saw your grandmother weeping because of her father and mother," Finn said. "We thought we'd better not upset her?"

"That house," Veronica said slowly. "It's said to be haunted, right? I remember that; Grandma's aunt hanging herself and the house being difficult to sell and all. You mean this wasn't the same body?"

"No. It was a grown woman, and we think it's Catherine, Alice's nanny," Sarah said, adding quickly, "Judging by the period of the woman's clothes."

"I hope you called the police."

"We did, and they already removed her body."

Veronica's lovely dark eyes suddenly became stern. "I'm sure you don't think my great-grandmother had anything to do with it?"

"No, but that's not everything," Emmie said. "I'm not sure if you know anything about this, but we found a voodoo doll that someone placed in with the woman's body."

Finn stepped forward and showed Veronica the photo on his phone.

"A voodoo doll?" Veronica's gaze once more jumped from one to the other. "That's odd."

Close to the counter and to Veronica now, Finn said in his special velvety tones, "Maybe you can give us some insight as to its origin."

"Do you mean because of the Arcane Temple in town? So you're thinking they might have had something to do with it?"

Emmie masked her confusion. She'd never heard of anything called Arcane Temple.

"Yes," poker-faced Finn said quickly. "Them. Exactly."

Veronica chuckled. "I hardly think they're capable of murder. Just a bunch of fanatical wannabes searching for a little attention —and money from those who believe in such things."

"So you don't think they're dangerous?" Sarah asked.

"Dangerous? God, no. There aren't very many of them in the group, from what I've heard, but they're more bark than bite when it comes right down to it. They stand on street corners sometimes, placing offerings, but I rarely see anyone talking with them. To most of us in town, they're a joke."

Emmie thought of the doll and the body again. That wasn't a joke, and it could not be coincidence that there should be a voodoo cell in a small place like that. Didn't they normally belong in sunnier, wetter climates? Haiti, or New Orleans?

"Besides, you're talking of a murder and a voodoo doll from how long ago?" Veronica shook her head dismissively, but she stopped and gasped. "Although..." They waited, and Emmie could swear her friends were not breathing, and neither was she. Veronica stood there with her head tilted. Her words came slowly. "There was a young woman murdered about ten years ago in this area. They found a voodoo doll with her as well—I remember the details were quite gruesome."

"Do you remember how, or why, they were gruesome?" Finn asked.

Scrunching up a little nose, she shook her head. "God, no. And don't ask me. I was fairly young too, but it must be online, right?" She gasped again. "Oh, I remember her poor father! He was hunting for her killer years later."

Raising a finger, as if asking for a moment, Veronica rummaged around the desk, rifling through stacks of papers and folders, until she pulled out a flyer showing the photo of a pleasant, college-aged woman with brown hair and a beautiful smile. *Justice for Natalie,* the flyer read across the top. *Should murder go unpunished? How does our justice system deal with acts too horrible to describe?* It listed a website where people ought to get more information about a gruesome killing in their own town, as well as the contact info for the woman's father, Tommy Cooper.

"Is he still around?" Emmie stared down into Natalie's pixeled eyes.

Veronica cringed and shrugged. "They never caught who did it, so maybe. He was a single dad, and the killer was still out there. A doll, and voodoo might have something to do with the poor girl's death, but I think it's best that you to contact Mr. Cooper with any questions before getting fed misinformation from crazy locals."

She looked back at two large suitcases and a smaller bag on top about the size of a laptop. "I'm leaving soon for a trip to Los Angeles—City of Angels. My ride should arrive soon. Wish it was for leisure, but there's a conference I need to attend."

"We have to go too," Emmie said. "Thanks for your help. You know how it is, I'm also having trouble selling the house, like Daniel and Ruth, and stuff just keeps happening."

"Yeah, I get you." Veronica grinned. "I hope you find out what happened. Maybe..." Again, her gaze moved over their faces, and this time lingered on Finn. "Maybe you should get the police to handle this. Put two and two together. It's new information, isn't it? I mean, old information, but the voodoo doll could tie it all into something?"

"Sure, the police," Finn scoffed.

Veronica quickly put some products, sample-sized, into three small turquoise paper bags, and handed them over. "You were so kind to come over"—she wagged a finger—"even if you kept a murder hidden, but I want you to have some goodies from my line. Write to me, let me know how you like them." She smiled at Finn. "Or call me."

A taxi arrived outside the front door and the driver peered out at them. Finn got immediately busy helping Veronica with her bags as a smiley woman came out from the back of the store to take her place. Emmie and Sarah nodded at the new arrival, took the bags of cream and left.

They waved to Veronica one last time, just as she and Finn shook each other's hands for a little too long before she climbed into her cab and drove away.

Sarah nudged Finn as they stood by Emmie's car. "Don't forget to call and say how you liked the products."

He was pulling out the creams and reading the names. "Yes, Miss Veronica, the gardenia-lavender complex with pet—pep—"

"Peptides," Sarah said.

"It really worked on my crow's feet."

"Which you got from squinting at her legs." Emmie handed the flyer to Finn after they'd climbed into the car. "Would you mind calling Mr. Cooper?"

"Not at all." Finn dialed the number and stared at the floor, but turned back to Emmie a few seconds later with a curious look. "It's disconnected."

"Damn," Emmie said, "nothing but dead ends today."

"Not to worry." Finn opened his laptop and clicked his mouse for several minutes before sitting up. "Got it. Tommy Cooper, 721 Highland Street. A different phone number too. I even found an old newspaper article about him."

Emmie typed the address into her phone's GPS and drove the two and a half miles across town to Tommy's address as Finn read the article. She slowed the car and pointed when the address came into view. It was a small white rambler obscured by trees and shrubs, with a chain-link fence around its perimeter. A car sat in the driveway. "It's right there."

"Not an inviting residence," Sarah said.

"Just park on the street," Finn said.

Emmie parked a little further up and shut off the car. "Showing up at Grace Hyde's home with gifts was tricky, but this man has had to deal with a lot. I'm not so sure he'd want to talk about something so painful."

"I had the same thought," Finn said, still looking at his screen, "except the article here talks about Tommy Cooper being an outspoken critic of law enforcement's handling of the case after no firm suspects turned up. But justice is what we do, right? We could offer our help, without giving him all the *psychic* details, and after finding out where his daughter was killed..." Finn held out his hands toward the girls.

"We could try to talk with his daughter."

"I got this." Finn held up a finger, pushed his laptop aside, and opened his door. "Don't worry, I'll be respectful."

Before Emmie could stop him, Finn climbed out of the car with his phone and shut the door.

"I hope he doesn't upset the man," Emmie said. "He can be a little brash."

"But he knows grief, Emmie," Sarah said quietly.

"True."

Which was why, probably, Finn walked away from them, then paced along the side of the street while talking on his phone. He didn't like to show them his earnest side.

Finn acted out the conversation with his hands and posture, even running his fingers through his hair, his gaze fixed on the ground at one point. For a while, it looked as if they'd be heading home without any answers, but a short time later, he walked back to the car with a somewhat sad grin.

He climbed into the backseat again, looking a little ashamed rather than triumphant. Then he said, "Mr. Cooper will see us now."

❧ 13 ☙

Finn handed his phone to Tommy Cooper as they gathered in the living room. The guys sat on the couch while Emmie and Sarah occupied chairs across from them. The air was stuffy, and the walls were bare. Only one small, framed photo sat on a table by the window, but Emmie avoided looking at it, and so did the others.

All the blinds were closed as if the owner of the house preferred not to see the beautiful fall day outside, and the harsh overhead light gave the impression they were on stage.

Tommy was a tall, handsome man, with a friendly goofiness about his face, as if he'd laughed all his life, until recently. He brushed back his brown thinning hair and stared at the photo Finn had taken of Catherine. Zooming in on the corpse and then the doll, he turned to Finn with a sparkle of fear or wonder in his eyes. "It's voodoo, yes. Have you talked to anyone else about this?"

Sarah shook her head. "No. Well, just the police because we had to report the body."

Tommy nodded. "It's not the police I'm concerned about." He leaned back in his seat but didn't return Finn's phone. "I've been searching for my daughter's killer for ten years now."

"There was an article. That's how we found you," Finn said.

"So you know the police are useless. It was a horrible murder, but they found no good leads and after a while they just let it drop." He didn't wait for them to commiserate. He barreled right on like a machine gun, as if he had said a lot of these things many times or kept saying them in his head. "Whatever you read, that's just the tip of the iceberg. If you're only interested in the item you found, I can tell you that it's the sort of doll connected with voodoo in the area. You might have heard the term *vodouisant*? That's just a generic term for someone who uses voodoo, but a group around here adopted the religion and started a temple and everything. They don't like anyone to say they do voodoo, though. They object to the term because of implications and all. In town, they have what is called the *Arcane* Temple, but it's a euphemism. They believe in magic, period. *Potayto, potah-to,* is what I say."

"And people here are all right with that?" Finn asked.

"They're within their rights. Religious freedom, like the Wiccas. Before, they couldn't have temples, but they're a branch that's been around for a long, long time in this area of the Midwest. You say the police have the item now?"

"Yes." Emmie nodded once.

"Better for you." He looked at Finn's photos again. "And I see the ring finger is missing from the woman's corpse. That happened to my Natalie." A pained look crossed his face.

Finn accepted his phone back and scrutinized his photo, then looked up at Emmie and Sarah, his eyes wide. His expression revealed that what Tommy was saying was true. "It's gone. We hadn't noticed."

"I'm not surprised," Tommy went on. "It's easy to miss a minor detail like that. But all the parts of the puzzle lead back to voodoo. The doll you showed me and the one found with Natalie match the characteristics of the ones they use in their rituals; the severed ring finger must have a connection with magic in their eyes. I know for a fact voodoo uses human blood in ceremonies, like a baptism is to Christians. But the worst part, what makes it more difficult, is that most of them are actually nice people. They take the light side of voodoo: protection, help, health." He nodded a few times. "You can bet, though, that a small number of them like the dark side. The power, the hexes, the love magic, the revenge magic, the blood rituals. And sometimes it's hard to tell who is who."

Tommy leaned forward and paused before continuing.

"Natalie was a good girl, a smart girl, and she was leaving a restaurant in town on October twenty-sixth, the place where she worked. It was late, just past one a.m. according to the restaurant's records for when she punched out, and on her way to her car she just disappeared. She never got there."

Finn's gaze dropped to the floor as he shifted in his chair.

"They even sliced off a chunk of my girl's hair," Tommy added.

At this, Finn looked up at Emmie, who blinked to let him know she remembered. The braid of hair they had found at Betty's; they would have to read more about what it meant: hair, cutting the ring finger—

"She was completely drained of blood," Tommy added in a strained voice. After a moment, he gestured to Catherine's picture. "Hard to tell if that happened to her, I guess?"

"But"—Finn cleared his throat—"how could there not be a lot of evidence left somewhere..."

His voice trailed off before Tommy went on with glazed eyes. "Where? Do you think a devil who does such things, things that require preparation, will do it out in the open?"

"Even where they left her, there must have been traces..." Sarah suggested softly.

"The dump site, they call it." Tommy gnashed his teeth, and for a mad second it looked almost as if he were about to laugh. "That's what they call it. Where they dumped my girl." Now he did laugh. "Ha! What did they get from it? Nothing. Just Natty and the doll. She wasn't naked, at least."

He stood up and took a crumpled pack of cigarettes from a shelf. That's why it smelled stale in there. Emmie hadn't seen anyone smoke, especially indoors, in so long that it seemed strange. Perhaps he had started after Natalie died. But although he fingered a cigarette as he thought with a scowl on his face, he didn't light it.

"They did an investigation," he said then. "I managed to get a copy of the paperwork, but they did a sloppy job. They even floated the possibility of a botched robbery because of the missing finger... As if anyone will bother to remove all the blood from a girl, somewhere else, then dump her, cut off her finger, leave a doll, just to steal a ring." Tommy chuckled bitterly. "She wasn't wearing a ring, anyway. She had no rings."

"So the police never had any suspects?" Emmie asked.

"They questioned a few people; I don't think that it was for any good reason. Boys she knew, people who worked with her, people from the voodoo cult. They all had alibis, so the police ran out of leads, and that's where it's sat for ten years."

Finn stirred. "So they didn't suspect the voodoo or *arcane* cult?"

"They did for a bit, but said there was no evidence to connect them to the murder. What about the doll? The finger missing?"

Emmie's throat hurt as she watched the veins bulge on his neck while he talked. He calmed down by rolling the cigarette between his fingers, still without lighting it.

"The Arcanists aren't considered dangerous, just eccentric. The police looked into them in a half-assed way and dismissed them. I will tell you what, though, someone in there took it *very* personally after I shared my opinions with the local newspaper."

Sarah leaned forward. "What did they say?"

"Didn't say anything, but I've found blood on my door, and symbols scratched across my car."

"Did you call the police?"

"Hard to make the cops understand who is doing it and why,

so I installed cameras recently. I'll catch them one of these times."

Tommy gestured to Finn's phone.

"I'm not sure the photo you've got is evidence of the original cultists back in the early days when it started. The sick bastards who killed Natalie are just copycats trying to revive the old practices. That's the short answer."

"What's the long answer?" Finn wondered.

Tommy stared at him for a few seconds without expression. But he wasn't getting angry; he stood up and gestured for them to follow him. "I'm afraid it would take me a while to tell you everything, but I can see you're serious about this, so I'll give you a taste of what I'm dealing with."

They followed him to a room that had obviously been Natalie's, judging by the blush/gold throw pillows and comforter over the twin bed in the corner, and the words 'Live Laugh Love' sprawled across one wall, with each letter created from photos of young sports celebrities. "Natalie had only moved out of the house a couple of months earlier before she was attacked. Our life fell apart, then my wife left me a few years ago. It's what often happens when couples lose a child—isn't that funny?"

He had transformed the bedroom into an office. It was well organized, with stacks of papers, folders, and filing cabinets.

Tommy stood in the center of the room, still mulling things. "The only other person who can feel a pain like yours is the person who also lost a child, but two people have different ways of coping. My wife finally chose to move on and me..." He held out his arms. "Everything you see in this room is related to Natalie's death in some way. My wife thought it was morbid."

Not that it wasn't. Some of the folders bore police department logos, and there were old VHS tapes, yellow pads covered with notes—some in frantic handwriting with arrows pointing up and down to other things, parts crossed and others underlined.

"I'm not in this room every day," he said suddenly, as if that might be the thing to label him as a madman. "Not like in the beginning. But sometimes, yes. Still." He held up the cigarette he had been holding. "My wife hated me to smoke in here."

Finally, he put the cigarette to his lips and lit it, and pulled an ashtray with a few butts already in it from under a stack of paper. He gave a small shrug and a little smile at the same time. He didn't appear to be challenging his wife or disrespecting his daughter. Just that it made no difference in either case.

Emmie caught Finn's glance at a corkboard on the wall. A bedsheet was draped over it so that only a few inches of one side were visible. He frowned at it, and now both of them were curious about it, but Tommy took a deep drag of the cigarette, let the smoke out and said, "There was another one."

Finn swiveled. "Another—?"

"Murder. It matched the methods used on Natalie. It happened about twenty years ago in a town an hour and a half away: a young woman named Jackie Swanson."

Rummaging in the stack, he found a police file and handed it to Finn.

"You can keep it if you want. I have digital copies. I digitize everything. Look at it and tell me if I'm wrong to think that there's a method to the madness."

Moving to Finn's side, Emmie and Sarah read it over his shoulder. It detailed a young woman whose body was dumped, bloodless, together with a voodoo doll. She had a syringe puncture mark on her neck and was missing her ring finger.

When Finn lifted the page, the photograph of Jackie Swanson was there. She looked pale as wax, her skin sticking to the bones of her face and arms, the puncture mark dark purple on her neck. Finn stopped on the close-up of the hand with the missing finger. Sarah gagged and turned away.

Another photo showed a doll; it was different from Catherine's. An updated version for the twenty-first century?

Finn closed the file.

Emmie wanted to ask Tommy for Natalie's report and

whether all the details matched, but considering that enough things did, she was going to assume so.

"The police didn't see this as a serial killing?" Finn asked in disbelief.

Tommy shrugged. "They know it's connected. The police of the two cities talked to each other. There was an effort at the state level. These aren't closed cases, you see." He put out his cigarette and shoved his hands in his pockets. "They investigated, but they had no leads. The cases are open, and they went cold."

"Do you mean it's all just going to sit there unsolved?" Sarah asked. "Two young women..."

"Two in twenty years," Tommy said, and shrugged again. "Not urgent enough, if there isn't more killing. A predator that might strike at any moment. One murder twenty years ago, another ten years ago. Like I said, cold cases."

Emmie's eyes scanned the tapes stacked vertically on a shelf beside the desk. "And what do you look at? I mean, how do you try to solve it?"

Tommy glanced at the corkboard. "There are surveillance tapes. I got the surveillance from businesses around the places where Natalie walked. She had her routine: home, school, work. Sometimes the gym. I gathered what I could from people who were actually filming the streets and places and not just pretending to. I've looked at them hundreds of times, thinking she must have been stalked; that the murderer is in those tapes. I know he is in there."

"You never saw any voodoo people in them?" Finn asked.

"Not so far, but I don't know them all," Tommy said. "And the police couldn't either. The difference is that they have dropped this, but I won't. I'll keep on looking."

A moment of silence passed between them.

"Thank you, Tommy," Finn said finally, handing back the file. "We won't take up any more of your time."

"Keep it, keep it. I have copies. I'm not supposed to have

them, though, so don't leave it lying around." Tommy grabbed a notepad and scribbled his phone number on it. "Call me if you find anything else. If I can help. Maybe you can help me too."

Tommy walked them out, and in the living room Emmie stopped by the photograph near the window. It showed Tommy and a soccer coach standing beside Natalie, and she looked younger than in the flyer he had spread around town. She was in a high school soccer uniform, her hair in a ponytail. The picture of innocence and joy.

"That's Natalie." Tommy smiled, apparently now able to talk about her.

"She's so pretty," Sarah said. "Did she like sports?"

"Loved them. She spent a lot of time on the soccer field and wanted to do it professionally. I'm confident she could have done it. She could have done anything."

Sarah turned and with that way she had, of knowing the right thing to do and the right time, she embraced Tommy. "Thanks for meeting us, Tommy."

He nodded, his face near hers. "Thank you for coming." He shook Finn's hand next. "Come back anytime."

Shaking Emmie's hand too, he walked with them to the door. The air was cool and fresh when he opened it, and they stepped out. Before they left, they turned to wave at him and he looked somber.

"The dark-voodoo people," he said grimly. "They seem like a joke to everyone. But don't fool yourselves and don't forget: One of them is a monster."

❧ 14 ❧

The words of Tommy Cooper echoed through Emmie's mind during the long drive back to drop Finn off at Caine House. Sarah had brought up a good point, that if the dark Arcanists were so dangerous that even an intelligent guy like Tommy Cooper feared them, then maybe they should investigate what they'd found with stealth.

"We can help the man get closure," Sarah had said, "even without forgetting to focus on getting help for Alice and Catherine."

"Agreed," Finn said in a quieter tone than usual. "Like him, I'm sure the cases are connected somehow."

"Too much coincidence," Emmie said. "And the thing in common is this school of voodoo: the ritual of the blood, the missing finger and the doll. We definitely need to know more about all that."

"Betty's books will only get us so far, I think," Finn said. The police report of Jackie Swanson's murder was rolled between his hands. He was obviously dying to dig into it without Sarah nearby. "We need field research, as they say. We need to go places and see people."

"The people we've been warned against, though," Emmie

said. They were reaching Caine House soon, and she needed to impress caution upon him. "He said it's hard to tell the dark ones."

She was glad to see Finn had recovered his smirk.

"That's not how it's done, civilians." He winked at them as he gathered his laptop and jumped out of the car. "Don't run over any black cats now. That's bad luck."

He waved to them from the front steps as they drove away.

And less than an hour later, in front of Hanging House, a sight sent Emmie's heart racing again.

Someone had painted a strange symbol on the front door.

Vandals?

No, and not red paint either. "Blood," she said.

"Oh, my God, Emmie."

Sarah stared at Emmie as the headlights revealed an odd symbol written across her doorway. It was a couple of feet wide and a few feet tall. A hexagon stretched out in the shape of a coffin with a star just above where the head would be. Its connection with death was unmistakable. "Just like Tommy said happened to him!"

Emmie didn't answer, but shut off the car and climbed out to get a better look.

"The voodoo people know about us? They know where we live?" Sarah said breathlessly.

Hell, yes. Emmie's heart had not settled, and she instinctively looked around the area as if the culprit might still be watching them from a distance. Nobody in sight. The blood was still dripping down the side of the wood frame around the door. There were no lights on in the house, just the way they had left it, but Emmie hesitated to approach it.

She had faced so many terrors within Hanging House, but the sight of that symbol had rattled her confidence. "Keep an eye out."

Emmie cautiously approached the front door. Standing on the steps, she took out her phone and snapped a picture of it.

She would send it to Finn as soon as she could, but now was not the time for a distracting text conversation. She needed to focus on the perceived threat.

The door handle had no blood on it. Maybe they hadn't gotten into the house, but the bigger problem stopped her from going inside. If a skilled occultist had created the symbol, there was no telling the dangers they might be in after passing through its center. "We can't go in this way, at least not yet."

"Do you think someone cursed the house? What if it's just a Halloween prank by some kids?"

"Nobody's laughing, but better safe than sorry." Emmie led Sarah around to the side of the house. Maybe Alice would be there to greet them, wondering why they were coming in through the side door. Could a ghost be affected by something that was obviously voodoo? Catherine's mouth sewn shut as a spirit to match the doll was proof that it could.

They checked the side door for any symbols like the one on the front, but it was just like it had always been. And it was locked—a hopeful sign that nobody had gotten into the house. She dug out the key, and they went inside.

The basement stairs were straight ahead, just by the door. Staring down into the darkened space, she wished she would see Alice. The girl would know if someone had entered the house while they were gone.

Never around when I need you.

"Should we call John?" Sarah asked.

"I'm not sure what he would do in this case. He might not be moved by the assumption that rowdy teenagers did this. But if anything happens, I'll race you to call 911 first."

"Got it."

Emmie opened the door to the kitchen a little more quietly than normal and stepped to the counter, grabbing the largest kitchen knife she could find. Sarah did the same, holding it out in front of her and whispering, "I'll cut your heart out."

At Sarah's humor, Emmie's mood lightened a bit. Maybe they

were making too much out of it, but their previous run-ins with a sorceress and the world of magic put her on edge. The symbol was occult, no doubt about it, but without knowing who had done it or why, she couldn't relax.

They moved through the living room and turned on all the lights along the way. If there were any intruders nearby, Emmie intended to flush them out. Walking over to the stairs going up, she yelled, "If there's someone in here, we're armed and we're not afraid to shoot."

Emmie glanced at Sarah. Her friend swallowed while staring back with wide eyes and a gaping mouth.

"I don't sense any strong feelings," Sarah said. "Maybe the curse or spell didn't take."

Lowering her knife, Emmie ran up the stairs anyway, with Sarah following closely. "Maybe you're right. Dammit, Alice, where are you?"

They searched each room and closet, the attic, then dashed downstairs and hurried to the back apartment before running to the basement. No sign of anyone, Alice or Catherine included.

"We don't know for sure that it's human blood," Sarah said. "It could be pig's blood. Human blood is actually difficult to get, unless you get it yourself."

"You're probably right." Emmie took a deep breath.

"We're just scaring ourselves now."

"That's all I ever seem to do in this place."

Sarah glanced around. "I wonder if Alice is open to talking with us yet."

"Oh, that reminds me, I better get Alice's music box out of the car. She'll be happy I returned it as promised."

They climbed the steps toward the kitchen, but Emmie stopped near the top. An icy chill shot up her spine. Someone had painted a symbol above the side door near the ceiling—on the inside and smaller, but it matched the symbol on the front door.

"They got in," Sarah said.

"Someone out there knows we're investigating the murders." Emmie's fingers trembled as she took a photo of the second symbol and texted both to Finn. "He should know about this."

A short time later, Finn returned her text with a quick reply. "A quintessential hexagonal," he wrote, followed by: "It means death."

🎇 15 🎇

*H*air: a very personal item. Like a fingerprint, like skin that could not as easily be cut off, it identified a person unmistakably. Teeth and bones could do the same, but could only readily be obtained after death. At times, spell casters didn't want to open corpses, or wanted to throw a hex on people without their knowledge; so hair was best.

Blood: precious life force. If consumed after the quick death of a victim, it would imbue the spellcaster with the attributes of the dead person.

The ring finger: signified promise or marriage. Could tie a person to the spellcaster and enchant them.

Bones: could be used for divination or enslavement.

And, a mouth sewn with twine denoted secret-keeping and silence.

EMMIE AND SARAH SAT TOGETHER ON THE COUCH THE NEXT morning reading an old book they'd pulled from Betty's basement. It had an unassuming cover and all of it was written by hand with the information laid out in painstaking penmanship and blue ink. The author had not published and shared this with the public for obvious reasons. It was dark voodoo. *Macumba,* Emmie's Brazilian ex-boyfriend would have said, believing fully in its power.

Hair, blood, the ring finger, bones. That was the gist of the items connected with the murders, but the book didn't detail any spells, as the writer's intentions must not have been for people to cast any. Which was all right and fine, except that Emmie would have been glad to cast a counter spell against the hex on their door.

"I suppose we could have guessed most of this," Sarah said, leaning back.

"And Finn must have been looking at this." She tapped a drawing in another book, a regular hardback this time, but of the kind she recognized as a limited edition. There was the same drawing, Fig.i, and some variations. "It's a warning, but also a threat. And yes, pretty much 'Leave me alone or die.'"

"Can't be worse than she who must not be named," said Sarah, meaning Josephine. "And we are stronger now."

Sarah was courageous for someone small, slight, and sensitive. But she also had great powers. The thing was that Emmie wasn't sure if their reading more about their powers since they'd received Betty's books and practicing a little really made them a match for dark voodoo experts.

On the other hand, why bother to leave a warning? Why not just kill them if they were getting close to some uncomfortable truth?

Besides, what choice did they have now? Even if their triumphing over Josephine and Victor had been a fluke, well, they'd just have to repeat the fluke.

Emmie called Finn just after breakfast and confirmed they'd spend the day investigating the murders separately to speed the process. The previous night's threat had thrown them into high gear and wasting time now wasn't an option.

"We'll visit Natalie Cooper's 'dump site' first," Emmie said. "I hope we have better luck with her than we did with Daniel at Hyde House."

"I won't be too far away," Finn said. "I want to stop by Tommy Cooper's house again. He's got *way* too much on his plate. It'll take him another ten years just to view all those surveillance videos he had stacked around his office. I've done this sort of thing before—I know some tricks to scan them a lot faster. Nobody should have to deal with a tragedy like that all alone. We'll meet at a later time to compare notes. Just one question."

"What's that?"

"How will you get along without my sweet face to brighten your day?"

Emmie grunted and laughed. "Somehow, we'll manage." She hung up without allowing him to throw out another wisecrack.

They found the exact location in an article about her death online, and forty-five minutes later Emmie followed the map on her phone to a park on the far side of Summerton, only a couple of miles from Tommy's house. Pulling into the parking lot, they saw no sign of anyone else nearby, either in spirit or physical form. It was early, and the weather was a little too chilly. People would probably start to walk their dogs or bring their children to play soon.

Emmie pointed to a line of tall grass beyond a gazebo. "That must be the creek. Natalie was placed on some rocks in a bend of the creek, though not in the water."

"Something feels odd," Sarah said.

Emmie scanned the area for any spirits but found none.

The weather must have been much the same back then as it was now, which would have delayed decay a little longer than summer weather. But according to the reports, she had disappeared in the early hours of the twenty-sixth and been found on the morning of the twenty-seventh, giving someone plenty of time to move her. She might have only lain outside for a few hours. And whoever had brought Natalie to that park ten years ago had taken her life, dumped her, then slipped away into the night like a pro.

"How did it happen...?" Emmie mumbled.

Arriving at the gazebo, they saw the water and carried on. Some of the branches overhead were bare and the dry, fallen leaves scattered over the grass crunched under their feet as they took a path and followed the creek's bend.

Despite the path becoming more secluded as they went, they weren't too far from a busy section of town. Just beyond a line of pine trees at the edge of the park was a row of retail shops and city streets. "Not exactly the most discreet place to leave a body," Emmie said. "Even if the killer dumped Natalie at night and the shops were closed."

"I agree. It makes me think..." Sarah hesitated. "It makes me think the killer wanted her to be found. At least, not wanted her to stay missing long."

"You mean he was merciful? Didn't want the family to wait and suffer?"

"Yes. Like it wasn't personal, you know?"

"You're picking that up, or...?"

Sarah shrugged. "It's a deduction. Otherwise, why would they risk coming here rather than throwing her inside a faraway body of water or in some woods? Isn't that what they usually do?"

Emmie shrugged. "You have to ask Finn."

The creek snaked away from town. There were bends hidden enough from view, especially at night, to allow a murderer to leave his work unnoticed.

"There is an odd feeling here," Sarah said behind her in a faint voice. Emmie turned to find her head lowered as she swayed a little. "I feel... disoriented. Isn't that weird? Someone's presence is here. And yet... they're not."

Emmie scanned the trees, paying attention to any dark areas where a spirit might hide from her, as children's spirits sometimes did. But this wasn't a frightened child. Natalie *should* appear.

She stepped over to the creek and stared down into the gently flowing water.

A panicked white face stared back at her.

Natalie.

16

Natalie's face appeared beside Emmie's. Not within the water, but on the water's surface—the young woman's reflection hovered silently. A chill ran up Emmie's spine as she looked beside her, into the empty space where Natalie should be.

At the same time, Sarah let out a loud groan—almost a scream—then stood up suddenly. Holding out one hand toward Emmie and the other over her chest, she winced as if a knife had pierced her heart. Her eyes stretched wide open. "Emmie..."

Emmie hurried to her side. "What's wrong?"

Now Sarah screamed. "It hurts!"

Sarah folded forward, clutching her chest, and toppled to the ground.

"Oh, God!" Emmie dropped to her knees beside Sarah. "You need a doctor."

"No. No, I don't. It's her. Don't you see her?"

"I saw her face in the stream."

Sarah had hardly ever reacted so strongly unless something big was happening, and it scared Emmie. Sarah must have sensed her fear, because she reached out and took Emmie's hand, even as she winced and moaned.

Emmie pressed her eyes together and focused intensely on

Natalie. If she was there, where the hell was she? The woman's *essence* was there. For sure, she had seen her face. No doubt she was tied to this place, where her body had been found, but somehow her spirit was somewhere else at the same time. Was it possible she could be attached to two different places? Could it be where she had been murdered? Emmie pulled on Natalie's essence, but a wall of darkness prevented her from connecting with the murdered girl's full spirit.

Sarah clenched her teeth and motioned with her head. "Let's go."

Emmie helped her stand and held her up as they moved back to the car. Sarah tensed and folded forward again, then let out another brief scream followed by a string of curses.

"I hate to put you through this." Emmie paused and brushed back her hair.

"Did you communicate with her?"

"No. I couldn't keep her around."

In the car, Sarah leaned against the passenger side door. She gasped for breath but appeared to recover. "I don't know what's happening to me. I haven't felt that much pain since before I had my appendix taken out. What do you think is happening?"

"I'm guessing she's manifesting the rage about her murder. But I can't explain why I couldn't see her spirit. Back in the house, I didn't see Daniel clearly either, just a glimpse of him. I haven't developed my psychic abilities enough to see all adult spirits yet, though. And then there is the doll, with the mouth sewn shut, like Catherine."

"They can't communicate, it seems," Sarah said. She was pale and rubbed her stomach, but she seemed better. "But they can lash out."

"Maybe we shouldn't visit Natalie's grave," Emmie said. It had been their plan.

"You always say ghosts are never there."

"She was here, at a dump site. Who knows whether this voodoo stuff makes their spirits different?"

"We should go anyway," Sarah said. "I'm better now. She won't take me by surprise if she's there, and we're running out of options."

Along the way, Emmie stopped to pick up coffees and some food for lunch. The hot drinks helped warm them as they sat beside Natalie Cooper's grave while trying to understand what had just happened at the young woman's dump site. At least the cemetery was serene, with no sign of Natalie or any spirits, as expected, and the golden and brown trees calmed them. Yet Sarah's face showed that she hadn't gotten over the disturbing ordeal near the river.

"I swear, it was like someone cutting into my chest." She pressed her hands over her heart. "Natalie was in pain, but it wasn't until I tried to connect with her feelings that the spirit attacked me. Could it be someone else?"

Emmie's mind jumped back to her brief encounter with Daniel in Hyde House. "Who, for example?"

"I don't think it would be anyone trying to protect her. There was a lot of anger in the spirit."

"Her face was not angry," Emmie said, liking the idea that whatever had attacked Sarah was something else.

"Natalie's in a lot of emotional pain. That was very clear to me. But it's becoming clearer that was another spirit standing in the way. I felt like that spirit could get to me, maybe even kill me if it wanted to, like it already had me and all it needed to do was squeeze its fingers together and crush me."

Sarah's eyes were lost, and she was speaking in a monotone. Emmie remembered when she had been possessed by Josephine. Could she have opened herself to whatever was out there? But as she leaned forward, Sarah blinked and gave a small laugh.

"Don't be afraid," Sarah said. "It's me. It won't be so easy for any spirit to do that again."

"Good. Though wouldn't whatever possessed you say that?"

Giggling, Sarah took her hand. "Silly, it's me." She frowned, processing a thought. "It's got to be connected to what happened last night. I remember reading in a book I brought home how to confront violent spirits..."

"I've met several over the years, but it's hard to know how to react without knowing what this other spirit is capable of. I think we should find out more about whoever left the marks on our doorways."

Emmie also thought of what she had been reading that morning in Betty's book: something about a ritual based on the lunar cycle. She pulled out her phone as Sarah watched her curiously. New Moon Healing; yes, she could remember that much.

A search for it returned some dead ends, touristic festivals, and one page that was apparently more serious. "*The New Moon Healing evokes a connection with the gods Obatala and Yemanja,*" she read.

Still frowning, Sarah followed her reasoning. "A ritual based on the moon when it's black?"

"Something very important, I guess." Emmie scrolled on the page to see that the link she had followed had led to an article that talked of the Summerton Arcanists, the nutcases Tommy Cooper had mentioned during their visit. A photo showed the group's temple, and there were quotes from a spokesperson, although the piece was from several years earlier. The address was below it.

"We can go there now." Sarah's expression was determined, not scared or in pain. She got to her feet.

Emmie followed suit.

On the way back to the car, Sarah rubbed her stomach again, smiling. "I've had patients hit me harder than this."

They left the area, and a few blocks from their destination, they started spotting people here and there dressed in white. It could not be a coincidence, as they all seemed to be walking in the same direction. Some crossed the street to greet others and hug them, exclaiming over their appearance as if they hadn't seen each other in a while.

Another group of women in white appeared down the block, and then a family climbed out of a car.

Who dresses in white in October Minnesota weather? Apparently, dozens of people who could only be going to... a temple?

Emmie parked a block away, and they stepped out of the car as more white figures shuffled past them.

"What's happening?" Sarah asked as they looked at each other. "Is it a special voodoo day?"

A moment later, Emmie spotted a flyer stapled to a pole.

~

Char Goodman
High Priestess of Summerton Arcane Temple

~

THE PHOTO ON THE FLYER SHOWED THE TEMPLE AND BELOW that, in the largest letters:

~

LUNAR STILLNESS
Observation October 6th

~

"THAT'S IT!" EMMIE GESTURED AT IT. "THAT'S THE SAME LINE Betty had underlined in her book. And that's two days from now."

Emmie discreetly ripped the flyer from the pole and carried it with her into the crowd.

The flow of people led them along the sidewalk toward a towering, old wooden structure ahead that could only be the Arcane temple. It was just as she'd seen in the article's photo, although larger than she'd imagined, and they must have constructed it at least a hundred years earlier, judging by its anti-quated structure.

The happy, chattering people filtered down to a single line as they all crossed through a metal gate, painted blue, and climbed the steps into the building. Its massive front doors opened wide to welcome the guests, and two tall men stood, one on each side of the doors, to greet them as they came in.

Emmie and Sarah weren't dressed in white like the others, and that earned them a couple of looks, but not unfriendly ones. More like curious, as if the person might be idly wondering what they were doing there.

They walked in with the others at the tail end of the crowd, and when the doors to the temple shut behind them with a boom, Emmie jumped. The sharp echo sounded so *final*.

But another sound filled the air. Rhythmic drums and clatter from musicians inside a large room to the right. In a small group, they banged drums with one hand and a stick. Two women danced around a small pile of scattered items Emmie didn't recognize. Several of the people who had just entered with them began to dance and clap their hands and joined that group. It was as if they were rehearsing.

The foyer where they stood had a high arched ceiling like a church, except the walls displayed tapestries done in the same unsophisticated style as quilts. Different scenes were depicted, some showing black people on tropical beaches. There were banners with animals, which changed from the large predators of the savannah to the more domesticated variety of cats, dogs, horses, and birds that could be found in America. She thought the men and women in the banners were gods of voodoo, like Bondhe, Brigitte, Samedi, Oshun: she remembered the way they were supposed to look from Betty's book. And from a James Bond film.

There were other scenes closer to home, of plantations and harvests. And the foyer itself seemed normal, a place with a corkboard announcing events and a display with lots of brochures that offered group activities like canoeing and choirs.

It was a mixture of the normal with the extraordinaire, but it didn't exactly inspire fear.

Until, that is, they kept walking straight ahead to the largest room, which turned out to be something like a theater or auditorium. But the stage was not in front, but in the center, and women dressed in white, some with white turbans and wide skirts, were arranging artifacts and objects, including candles, bowls, statues, and what seemed like rattles made of wood around it. A broad-shouldered woman who must have been at least six feet tall directed their efforts. From the rafters and the columns hung banners depicting the moon in its several stages of waxing and waning, with the new moon at the center, just facing them.

A large chandelier was on the ground and people were lighting the candles on it. Maybe not such a clever idea in a place made of wood?

Emmie considered leaving to try a smaller room where they might find someone less busy to talk to, though it seemed like an important day for the temple, and she had already taken Sarah's wrist to pull her away when the tall woman lost her grin, frowned, and then looked up, wide, green eyes zeroing in on Emmie with the precision of a missile. The woman's gaze jumped from Emmie to Sarah for several seconds before she let out a very loud, "Ah!"

The people with her paused their work and looked up at them as well, and Emmie and Sarah stood transfixed under their stares.

Pointing at them, the tall woman spoke commandingly in a booming voice, "Stop where you are! You have been hexed!"

✢ 17 ✣

Finn stood at the front door to Tommy's house. The doorbell camera stared back at him, and he pressed the lighted button in its center, then looked around while waiting for the door to open and spotted another camera in the corner above the garage. This guy was serious about security. Or about catching voodoo delinquents.

Holding his laptop under one arm, Finn tapped his fingers along its metal edge. He hadn't been able to get the thought out of his mind that there was this desperate father trying to find the murderer of his daughter and that he, Finn, had the skills to help the man. He couldn't let that go so easily. Tommy was buried in surveillance videos.

Finn noticed a dark red pigment along the doorframe. But the house was a light brown color, without any red accents. Stepping back, he could see that the red color circled the doorway. It was faded, barely imperceptible, but it was there. Yes, Tommy had been the recipient of a blood symbol, just like the girls.

Tommy opened the door, his hair a mess and his eyes tired. "Finn, thank you for offering to help. Please come in."

They went straight to the office. He had cleared off a side desk, and Tommy gestured to it. "You can put your laptop there, if you'd like, or anywhere you want. Maybe you'd rather sit on the couch?"

"Right here is fine." Finn set up his laptop and stared at the pile of tapes.

"Oh, don't worry," Tommy said quickly. "I told you, I digitized everything." He touched a large hard drive in a black case. "The drive is almost full. Eight terabytes. And you probably know how it is. Sometimes I go through it frame by frame. There's about a hundred hours of video on that one alone."

"OK, I'll start with that."

Finn plugged the hard drive into his laptop port and began the process of pulling it into the computer program that he had used so many times to process his own videos. He had developed a method of working with it, able to recognize the nonevents from the sudden flashes of light, and used a sophisticated software program to filter out the anomalies in the backgrounds. Any strange images or anything too different from the previous footage set off a notification that something was there. He could get through the video in a fairly short amount of time, as long as the aberrant objects in the video weren't moving all the time.

That process was for looking at paranormal activity, though. This time, things would be more tedious because he had to pay attention to people going about their normal, everyday business. Like Tommy, he didn't know what he would be looking for until he saw it. There would be no flashes of light or blue auras. Just people.

Tommy directed Finn to what he supposed would be the most relevant videos at first, the place where Natalie had worked. The camera of the restaurant faced the parking lot behind a small retail strip in town. The video started playing, and Tommy calmly pointed out Natalie among the people coming and going. She appeared driving a green car, got out, moved through the lot to the back door of the restaurant, smiling, greeting others, and disappeared inside.

There was a lot of activity in the early minutes of the video, with employees coming in and out of the back door to take smoke breaks, talk on their phones, and sit in their cars before driving away. Nothing unusual, and no Natalie.

The video was grainy and distant, some of the worst video feed Finn had ever seen, but it showed enough of the overall actions of people to get a clear picture of their purpose. Easy to follow them around, but no one stood out.

Finn had begun to think of the terabytes and how many of these he might have to watch, since they showed a lot of nothing interesting, when Tommy suddenly said, "There's more, you know."

"More what?" *Oh God, not more tapes!*

"Murders," Tommy said.

Finn swiveled in his chair and Tommy swiveled in his to face him. "Yes, murders. Just like Natalie's."

"I know," Finn said, frowning. "You told me about Jackie Swanson."

Shaking his head, Tommy rose and started pulling the bedsheet off the corkboard.

Finn gasped at seeing what Tommy had kept hidden.

A map of Minnesota and Wisconsin. Four red dots pinpointed locations on the map, and each had a wallet-sized photo of a woman next to it.

One of the photos was of Natalie. The other of Jackie. Finn walked over, his hands in his pockets, and waited for Tommy to explain.

"I thought you might dismiss me if I talked about four murders. Suggesting it was a serial killer doing this might drive you away, as it does most people when I bring it up, so I kept it to myself that day."

"Were they killed the same way?" Finn was looking from one photo to another, but something was off...

"They all died the same way as Natalie and that woman you mentioned in the basement of your friend's house. All had their blood drained and ring finger severed, and a doll with them."

Tommy pointed to each photo and listed the info for each of them. "Here is Shannon Peterson, found on October 27, 1981." He tapped another photo. "This is Audrey Catskill. Found on October 7, 1991. And then this young lady was Jackie Swanson, who I mentioned before, was found on October 16, 2001." He pointed to his daughter last and tapped the photo gently. "They took away my Natalie on October 26, 2011."

That's what he'd thought odd before. The young women's photos were from a time when people still printed them in shops, and their hairdos and makeup were outdated. Shannon had the big hair and frosted lips of the 80s, while Audrey had the heavier makeup of the 90s, with sleeker hair.

"Four murders, each of them ten years apart?"

"That's right. And always in October."

"And it's October." A chill passed through Finn. "You think the killer will strike again?"

"Who's to say? But the pattern is obvious." He reached toward a stack of papers and took a flyer from it. "They don't even hide it. They have their own Halloween, kind of. Lunar Stillness, they call it." He tapped the paper. "Always during the New Moon in October."

Finn read every word on the flyer. "Do the police know? I mean, this could be a reason for them to kill. More power from the killing or whatever they believe."

"Yes, they know. Even what you say, the Arcanists think this is a super powerful time. And there is my frustration: I've been trying to make the police see these deaths are connected, but they only see murders over forty years, plus mumbo-jumbo stuff, and just decide these are ritualistic killings from voodoo followers gone amok."

"Probably, but..." Finn shook his head. "The killers still have names and addresses and need to be behind bars. This is enough to get the FBI involved."

Tommy scoffed and reached for a cigarette. Once again, he only kept it between his fingers without lighting it. "The FBI got involved. At the third murder, Jackie. I couldn't get a hold of their report, don't know anyone there. When Natalie died, after a while they came and interviewed me. The suits, just like on TV." He gave a grim smile. "I was even a suspect for a bit."

"Everyone seems suspicious to cops," Finn said slowly, sitting down again. "That's because murderers usually originate near the victim."

"Yeah. I had an alibi."

Finn stared at the faces of the four young women. "They're all about the same age."

Tommy nodded. "That's another thing. But the murderer must be far along in age by now, if it's the same person. Even if he started killing young, in his twenties, he'd be old now. Maybe he's dead. Maybe this time October will pass without the killer acting on it because he's weaker."

"But maybe he has an accomplice. And it doesn't really explain Catherine's murder—the woman in the wall. Damn..." Finn said. "Considering Catherine and how similar her murder was, they've been doing this for a hundred years at least. It has to be a long line of people."

"Maybe people keep this moon sacrifice going, and there always will be a killer strong enough to do this."

Finn looked up at Tommy. "Then this killer is about to strike again. Two days."

THERE WAS NOTHING ELSE TO DO BUT TO KEEP LOOKING through the video feeds. At least nothing he could think of at that moment.

The two men worked in silence, occasionally taking a break to eat or drink something. Tommy even took the time to make them sandwiches and offered Finn a beer, which he reluctantly declined since it would interfere with his focus. Twice Tommy stepped outside to smoke, and each time he returned, the cold air rushing in through the back door would rouse Finn to attention.

It was after Tommy came back from his second smoke break and Finn hit play on a new section of video that he saw her.

This was a feed from the inside of Natalie's gym. Finn had seen Natalie running on the treadmill already, probably to keep her legs strong for soccer. And what he saw now, walking up to the treadmill next to hers, was a stocky female figure, inappropriately dressed in leggings, her hair and head hidden by a baseball cap. Her shoulders were hunched forward as she input her data into the treadmill's screen. Her body language showed her frustration with the machine, and Natalie, running next to her, pointed and spoke until the woman nodded and pressed more buttons.

Natalie laughed pleasantly as her ponytail bounced, and with shoulders still hunched, the stocky woman began her own exercise.

There was something oddly familiar about her. He fast-forwarded the feed until the woman left before Natalie had finished. He couldn't see the woman's face, but many gym members had a routine. Maybe the woman had returned the next day?

He kept forwarding the gym's feed until he found Nathalie again, around the same time two days later, going to the same treadmill.

And not long after, the stocky woman appeared, and this time Natalie smiled at her.

Finn zoomed in on the figure but only got the cap. There was always something wrong with security footage. Either a cheap camera, or poor angle, or the digital compression destroyed the image.

Always something. In this case, a camera above the gym and a woman who kept her face away from it.

He *would catch her*. He had an odd feeling about her.

Was it a woman who lured the prey so a man could kill her?

These duos were not unknown in serial murders: a dominant and a submissive. The woman appeared strong enough to drag Natalie about.

"Sure you don't want that drink?" Tommy asked, his voice exasperated.

"Huh?" Finn blinked. He'd better not seem like he had found something. Better not get Tommy's hopes up if it turned out to be nothing. "Uh, no. I'll just keep looking for a little while."

Tommy looked at the clock on the laptop, pushed his chair back, then stood up with a groan. "I'll have one for you."

Finn nodded politely, and after Tommy left, he went back to fast-forwarding the feed. Again, two days later, there they were. Same setup, and the two women were getting friendlier and friendlier.

"Why do you hide your mug, my beauty?" Finn murmured at the screen.

As Finn strained his eyes only inches from his laptop screen, the lights in Tommy's house flickered, dimmed, and then burst back to normal.

Tommy walked in holding an open bottle of beer, but didn't seem to notice the lights.

"Bad wiring?" Finn asked.

Tommy glanced around. "No, really new."

The lights flickered on and off again, never losing power completely, but stuttered as if someone were playing with the light switch.

"Strange," Tommy said, looking up, already at his desk.

Finn watched the nearest lamp. Probably just an electrical issue, maybe a downed pole or power surges, but still... he was used to the connection between flickering lights and paranormal activity.

He switched on his laptop's camera, capturing the view over his shoulder as he continued to work. Maybe it was nothing, but he would kick himself if he missed anything... unusual.

After flickering a little more, the lights returned to full power and Finn scrubbed through the video feed, playing it back a little faster until the figure appeared in the video again. Fourth time.

And it was only a matter of time, always, until people were careless. Because then Natalie arrived behind the woman and must have called out. The stocky stranger turned, and for a moment, the angle of her neck allowed him to see her face.

He gasped and stared, then went back, his eager finger pushing the arrow too far. He waited for the moment again, ready to pause. The neck tilted, and there was the face. He paused.

It took him a moment to process what he was seeing.

He threw himself back in his chair with his mouth hanging open. "Oh, my God. Of course. Of course, it was there, all the time."

Tommy swiveled in his chair, peering at Finn's screen. "What is it? Who's that woman? Do you know her?"

"Yes, we visited her yesterday. Zelda Hyde."

"You know her?" Tommy asked.

"I met her once, but she is connected to the house where Catherine's murder took place. It was her family home once, way back in time."

Tommy's mouth dropped open. "Are you serious?"

"I know for sure that it's a woman named Zelda Hyde. She's huskier now, if anything."

"Zelda Hyde," Tommy repeated.

Finn glanced at the corkboard, at the maps and the four photos, then turned back to his laptop. "And wait a second." He did an Internet search for Zelda Hyde. It wasn't such a common name, but of course there were still a few others. He checked the names against some profile photos on LinkedIn and found her. Zelda was a representative for big pharma medical supplies.

Medical supplies like... syringes? Gloves, body bags, and all sorts of goodies? Convenient profession for a murderer?

The smell of cigarettes on Tommy was a bit overwhelming as he leaned in next to him to see what he was digging up, but Finn scrolled down Zelda's resume until one word, black and bold, jumped out at him: Phlebotomist.

A nurse who draws blood...

Tommy must have understood the implications, since his eyes were filling with tears.

"She was with Natalie... The puncture marks in all the girls..."

"And if the police or the FBI look," Finn said softly, "she might have been in Wisconsin for the deaths of the other two girls, way back when. There will be some sort of record. Her work might have sent her there, or she might have lived there or used a credit card or stayed in a hotel... The point is, we have a name to give them, and then they can find out if she—"

Abruptly, Tommy stood and walked away as if deep in thought over the discovery. Facing away from Finn, he wiped his forehead with the back of his hand, then started trembling.

"You okay?" Finn asked. "I know this is probably overwhelming for you, but finally, we have something specific to tell the police. And it ties to Catherine's murder."

Tommy didn't react. Instead, he groaned and sputtered something under his breath. "It's... I... I... ca... ca..."

Finn stood and stepped toward him just as he turned around. His face was drained of color and his muscles twitched as he stumbled back to his desk and dropped into his seat.

"Are you all right? Should I call an ambulance?" Finn asked.

Tommy only stared ahead as if caught in a daze.

He's having a seizure. Tommy's hands trembled, and he clutched the arms of his chair. His body stiffened as if a low level of electricity was surging through him.

Finn tried to remember what to do in such a case. Have them bite down on something? Keep them from hurting themselves? He reached out to hold Tommy's arm.

Tommy snapped his hand around Finn's forearm and pulled.

"Tommy, let go. I need to call an ambulance." Finn looked back at his phone, sitting on the table next to his laptop.

The grip tightened around Finn's arm to the point where he thought the bone might snap. He held back a scream as the pain flooded his brain.

"Let go!" Finn cried.

Tommy did, and Finn tumbled to the floor.

Before Finn could get up, Tommy stretched his arms across the desk and ran his hands over a cup full of pens and scissors. Picking out the scissors, Tommy slowly turned and faced his guest. His eyes narrowed and his mouth closed as if he'd calmed down, but spit still dripped from the corner of his lips. Tommy's gaze was distant yet aware as his shoulders slumped and he lifted his chin. Something sparkled in his eyes, and his body shuddered again before submitting to whatever had taken hold of him.

Tommy raised the scissors, opened them, and pressed one of the blades against his throat.

"No!" Finn screamed. He tried to stand, but his legs went numb.

The man had stopped trembling as he moved the tip of the scissors across his throat slowly and firmly, with no more concern on his face than if he were opening a letter. The blood sprayed down Tommy's shirt and over at Finn as he sat frozen for a moment, watching Tommy's face. He couldn't look away. The man's blood kept spraying as the air escaped from his lungs within seconds.

Finn stretched out his hand, but it was no use. "Tommy, what the hell!"

As Tommy dropped the scissors and fell backward clutching at his neck, an icy stiffness passed through Finn's body. Not the icy chill of fear, but something deeper. The numbness spread from his legs up through his body and he struggled to breathe. Darkness crept over Finn's eyes like an eclipse, drowning more than the light as he gasped for air. Something was threatening to consume his consciousness, his reality. His muscles relaxed, and he wrestled with himself to stand and grab his cell phone, but his arms wouldn't cooperate. The darkness was winning.

The bloodied scissors lay only inches away on the floor in front of Finn, and they called to him. They looked... enticing.

You want them. You need them.

As if on autopilot, he reached out and picked them up.

This is what you get.

He raised the bloody blade to his own throat.

No. Finn pushed away his thoughts. *It's not me. Someone is controlling us.* Tommy still gagged and groaned.

Finn couldn't move forward or stop himself from pressing the knife blade of the scissors tighter against his throat. *Control.* He had read enough of occult practices to know he was under someone's spell. *It's not real,* he assured himself.

Tommy still gurgled above him and sagged forward in his chair. A lot of blood had drained out of him, and Finn still couldn't lift himself to get help.

The back door opened and slammed shut before someone walked into the room. Finn cried out, but the intruder laughed. A woman's laugh. She walked in wearing a bizarre flowery raincoat: red and pink flowers over a cheery yellow background. Finn found himself idly wishing that horrible garment wouldn't be the last thing he saw on this earth. She stepped over to Tommy and stared over at him with an annoyed expression.

Finn saw her face clearly. Zelda.

Tommy was still gurgling.

"You're not as easy to kill as your daughter was," she said. "Rest assured, her sacrifice was not in vain. I might have spared you if you had just minded your own business, but now all of your work is wasted."

Zelda clenched her fists, relishing Tommy's final moments of suffering until he collapsed in his chair and closed his eyes. She then turned to Finn.

The numbness in Finn's body faded as he struggled to gain his coordination. He floundered, but was sure he could get back to his feet. If only...

A jolt of pain hobbled him, just as he gained his footing.

A little more time and I'll knock the bitch to the ground.

She leaned down toward him. "Why can't you do as you're told? You saw what happened to your friend, so why do you make it hard on yourself? It's not my place to argue with the gods, but do you think you can defend yourself against Maman Brigitte? She has chosen you to fall asleep. I will put you to bed."

Some of Tommy's blood had spattered onto Zelda's raincoat and dripped down like wet paint. The raincoat's true purpose made sense now.

Practical woman, but it won't stop my fists when I...

Zelda glanced around the room with a scowl. If she picked up the scissors, he'd end up just like Tommy. Instead, Zelda picked up Tommy's massive external hard drive enclosure, unplugged it, and smashed it over Finn's head.

Everything went dark.

❦ 19 ❦

"Come up here, my sweet ladies, and let me help you free yourselves from that hex."

This was none other than Char Goodman, the priestess mentioned and shown in the flyer Emmie had taken.

Char extended a hand, beckoned, and stared at them without blinking. "What are you waiting for?"

Emmie stiffened and smiled nervously within the flood of attention from the upturned faces. "What hex?"

"Oh, I can see it around you. I think you know what I mean." She pointed to the steps leading down to the circular stage. "Both of you, step down here and let me heal your spirits. You cannot have a hex on you at a time such as this."

"How do you feel about her?" Emmie whispered to Sarah.

"I... think she's okay. Let's do it."

Emmie and Sarah walked down the carpeted steps to the stage. A heavyset woman was kneeling on the outside edge of a large circle made from a line of sand. She had gone back to her task, leaning into the circle, shifting around sand, candles, and cowrie shells as if trying to decide a place for each item. She was making patterns. There were also rattles and beads near her.

Char stepped over to Sarah. "It's a good thing I found you."

"We found *you*." Sarah had a puzzled look.

The priestess laughed. "Not true. The gods brought you here, and it's a good thing. You might not have survived two nights."

The Lunar Stillness? Today was the fourth, so it would take place two nights from now. Finn's interpretation of the symbols someone had painted on her doorway came back to her. *Death.*

Looking at Sarah, Char gestured toward the circle. "Step into the center. The hex has weakened you the most. Mimi, help her."

The kneeling woman, Mimi, broke her focus on the circle to guide Sarah into its center. "Please make yourself comfortable."

"What are you going to do?" Emmie asked Char.

"Just what I said I would—heal your spirits. The shadow of the hex has consumed your light."

Emmie noticed the white scarf draped around Char's shoulders and remembered reading that a priestess of voodoo would often wear a head covering during ceremonies so as not to be distracted by spirits. Char was covering her head now, and Emmie prepared herself to see spirits, but none appeared.

Char directed Emmie to sit in another small circle within the circle that Mimi was creating, just like Sarah's. She obeyed.

Mimi shifted the sand around with her hands and moved the shells and candles so they formed another layer of patterns inside the larger symbol. It wasn't a pentagram or another occult symbol, but it looked intricate. Emmie had seen such complex patterns, almost like lace, when leafing through Betty's voodoo books. She just didn't know what this one meant.

Lighting the candles one by one, Mimi recited something under her breath after each flame burned steadily. Once they were all lit, she sat upright and clasped her hands together with her eyes closed. The air was still.

Char looked at Sarah. "Take a deep breath, my child."

Sarah inhaled deeply with a nervous smile.

The kneeling woman picked up a bound circle of sticks, like a small wreath just a little larger than the woman's hand. A pentagram made of bones filled the center. It was tied to the sticks with something that looked like feathers. She lit them with a candle, waved the item in front of Sarah, who coughed, and chanted a long, drawn-out string of words in some sort of odd dialect. A moment later, a gust of wind rushed over them, and the candles fluttered before their flames went out.

Mimi turned sharply toward Char, her face full of fear. "It's Bade."

"What's Bade?" Emmie asked Char.

"He is the loa of wind." Char glanced up as if even indoors she might see the source of the wind's disturbance. "You need more than cleansing. You need protection." Char began opening bags that contained sand. "Do you believe in the arcane?"

"We... have come to believe." Sarah looked a little apprehensive, but she straightened her back, as if readying herself for what was coming.

Char looked anything but menacing; her smile was kind.

"Wise girls." Char used the sand to draw symbols around Sarah, but her symbols were more intricate than the ones Mimi had created.

Char turned and began creating the same ring of sand around Emmie.

"The hex on you is very powerful," Char said, as if she guessed their concerns.

"Someone drew a symbol around our doorways last night," Emmie said.

"Then, when you passed through the doorway, you invoked the hex." Char and Mimi nodded at the same time.

"Who would have done something like that?" Emmie asked. "Someone from this group?"

Pausing, Char glared at Emmie. "We do not do such things. Not this group. Our beliefs do not harm others, only protect. Do you remember what the symbol looked like?"

Emmie grabbed a handful of the sand, poured it on the floor and shaped the symbol with her fingers.

The priestess lurched forward in a panic and brushed it away before Emmie could finish. "You mustn't draw such things. Not ever."

"Sorry."

"... But I know the symbol you were trying to complete. It's malicious. Someone intended to do you great harm. I can tell you with certainty that nobody here would do such a thing."

Emmie nodded. "Who else would know how to do it?"

"There are others—not with us. But whether you love darkness or light, it is an important time for everyone now, as we all await the Lunar Stillness."

"What does it mean, the Lunar Stillness? Sounds... scary. I never heard of it before."

"It's not widely known, except in this area. In our origin we may have been inspired by Haiti, Africa—but things changed and adapted to this environment a little, maybe to farming, and to All Souls. A kind of merging of beliefs. You could say it's a bit of Wicca, and a touch of Native American witchcraft mixed with African and Haitian voodoo."

"I see. But then the hex..."

"Like every belief that offers power, this one has attracted people who want it for its sake. Even to make others suffer or control them."

"We met someone like that," Sarah said. "From New Orleans."

"Many came here from Louisiana, but a long time ago. In fact, in a way, our practices evolved to protect the settlers here from their dark power."

Emmie thought of Josephine and could well believe it. Hers had been a time when people from all over the country and beyond were rushing to this part of the country to have their opportunity, grab a piece of land, a mine, or become rich with trade. Whole towns had cropped up: this would have attracted a good many dark practitioners. Ambitious creatures like Josephine would want to escape the control of their mentors to rule over others with their powers. She had wanted to rule over a town, and probably keep increasing her reach.

Hadn't Betty been living in Minnesota because there was dark magic all around these apparently sleepy towns?

It was strange to have a pagan temple in a smaller city like Summerton, but magic practitioners must have been around for a long time, first in hidden cells, or even inside houses; women discussing spells as they made food in the kitchen, or meeting in barns, or washing clothes together in rivers or walking in the woods. Women who would exchange recipes to cure diseases and fevers, then spells for good harvests, then poisons. It might have started for good and then got twisted into evil, like so many things.

And today the world was about diversity, so they could be here and seem like harmless nuts. At worst, like people trying to get money out of others.

"Let's get you cleansed." Char started the ritual by directing a few women on the stage to take up the rattles and start shaking them. They sounded a bit like snakes. Two other women began to play tiny smooth drums.

The rhythms echoed around them, softly, at first, as Char stood over them. She started chanting in that same dialect again, and her voice had become husky and deep, as if someone else were speaking through her. She kept chanting and writhing to the beat. Her eyes had gone white.

It lasted for ten minutes, and then Char stopped abruptly, let out a long, rasping breath and stood still. Slowly, her pupils returned, and she blinked. Smiling down at Sarah, she took her hand, pulled her to her feet and led her out of the circle.

Sarah stared at Emmie with a warm smile. "I do feel different."

"It has been broken." Char nodded, helping Emmie up as well.

An aid approached, tapping down fragrant tobacco into a small pipe, and handed it to Char. Another woman gave her a shot glass full of clear liquid; it smelled like rum. Char puffed on the pipe several times and drained the glass, smacking her lips.

"I must smoke and drink to get the spirit who helped you out. It's payment and thanks." She let out a happy burst of laughter. "Sounds like an excuse to be bad, doesn't it?"

She puffed some more and considered the two women.

"Listen to me: You have enemies. And judging by the severity of the hex, you would be wise to protect yourself from further attacks by accepting a pwen doll Mimi will create for you to take home." She looked at her silent assistant, who immediately sat cross-legged on the ground and got busy with twigs, twine, feathers, and cloth.

"I thought they used dolls for... bad purposes?" Sarah said.

Char shook her head. "Not only. They can also protect. You've heard of amulets and gris-gris?"

The doll next to Catherine's body had not been made to protect, Emmie was sure of that. And if anyone could help them get answers about the whole magic aspect of the murders, it was Char.

"What if—" Emmie said. "What if we find a doll beside a woman's corpse? Like buried with her?"

Looking a little puzzled, Char nevertheless said, "It's hard to tell. It depends on what substance filled the doll. If the creator filled it with bones, for instance, then that might invoke Papa Ghede, the spirit of death, but a substance such as sand or flowers, or feathers, such as the one Mimi is creating for you, might invoke Papa Legba, the spirit of protection."

"Doesn't Mimi need anything from us?" Sarah asked, touching her hair and then her clothes.

Emmie swallowed. *Hopefully not bones.*

"No." Char smiled. "That's for the harmful ones. The one with the corpse you mention. Do you know what it was made of?"

"No."

"If you were the one who discovered this doll," Char said. "It might be why you had this hex."

It could be, or it could be the symbol.

"The doll had its mouth sewn," she told Char.

"Ah. Well, you can imagine what it means."

"Keep the dead person silent?"

"Yes. If you make a doll and use the person's hair and perhaps bones, and you clothe it with their cloth and sew the mouth shut, you are keeping a spirit quiet. A spirit like that knows secrets. Most often—"

"It was murdered," Sarah said quietly.

"That's it," Char said with regret. "The kind of thing that makes people afraid of what we do. In this part of the country, the doll was also merged with the dolls farmers used to have. Scarecrow type of thing. Or dolls that were used for land fertility. But what you described is a hex, and a bad kind. To keep a spirit roaming but quiet..." She now looked mournful. "It's a terrible thing. We should all find peace, don't you think?"

"We do," Emmie said. She would not tell this kind woman that it had become their life's work and the thing that had brought them there, and made them the target of malice and curses.

"What about a missing ring finger?" she asked as they slowly climbed the steps together.

"How horrible!" Char grimaced. "What this person must have gone through!"

"Yeah..."

"A ring finger means marriage, of course," Char said. "In our practice, we bless that finger for a fruitful, happy marriage. In dark practices... Well, we don't know all about the dark arts. They passed on much of it mouth to mouth, and only if the magician trusts the assistant. But removing a ring finger from someone is like stealing their ability to be a bride. Therefore, the person who stole it might be keeping a husband or wife hostage and obsessed by love. Unable to get away, although they might want to."

Who would need that, Emmie wondered. Catherine and young girls like Natalie and Jackie: clearly, pieces of them had been stolen for a purpose.

She jumped when Mimi appeared behind her, not breathless at all from running up the steps they had climbed slowly. She thrust two dolls at them and said in a matter-of-fact and very American tone, "There you go."

Each young woman took a doll, while Mimi turned to jump down the steps back to the stage.

They crossed the foyer with Char, and Sarah gestured to the crowd, which was now divided into several rooms or bustling about. "What's the significance of the Lunar Stillness gathering for everyone? It seems they have come from out of state, even?"

"Yes, they have come from all over the country. It's similar to winter solstice, except the tradition centers on the moon rather than the sun. It's a dark day, as the evil spirits are at their most potent. Our Halloween, if you will, except that there are no costumes or trick-or-treaters." Char smiled again. "We gather on this day each year to focus our strength on protecting the world from malicious spirits because it is a day when the dark ones can do a lot of harm."

Emmie shuddered and saw that Sarah had grown serious.

"And especially this year," Char went on.

Sarah's mouth opened a little as if afraid to speak, but then did: "Why?"

"Two nights from now will mark the Lunar Stillness decennial, a treacherous day every ten years for the world," Char said. "The usual protections do not bind evil spirits, so those with dark powers celebrate this day. They scatter among the world for the night to feed off the innocent."

A treacherous day every ten years... Why did that seem significant?

"... So it's especially important that you keep it with you at all times for the next evenings," Char insisted. "Don't forget."

"Wait," Emmie said, laying a hand on Char's sleeve. "Can you tell me more about what might happen two nights from today?"

"It was said that in olden times, the dark ones would find a virtuous spirit to slaughter and refresh their evil. It's a time of sacrifice. Some writings say that if they can't find a victim on the exact day, they will die. Without a sacrifice, their sins catch up with them. Understand?"

I understand too well. And judging by Sarah's expression, she did too.

Both Emmie and Sarah thanked Char before leaving the temple, but they broke into a brisk walk as they cleared the steps and the gate.

"A sacrifice," Sarah said.

"The girl whose death Finn is looking into, she died ten years before Natalie. And today is almost exactly ten years after."

"The moon won't be still, as they call it, on the same exact day every year," Sarah pointed out.

They took each other's hand without pausing, two young women holding dolls and each other as if this were child's play. Except that it wasn't.

"No," Emmie said. "It will be still two nights from today."

Finn pulled on the roots and clumps of dirt around him as
he sank back into the hazy darkness. A bird chirped nearby,
and he struggled to sit up, but cold, shadowy hands held him in
place. The descent into isolation continued as hazy images
flashed through his mind. A woman's voice, then a booming
thump, and the stillness didn't seem so bad after a while. It was
soothing, like his father calling his name.

But it wasn't his father, it was his brother, and he was
speaking to him from above somewhere in the darkness.

"Wake up, Finn," Neil's voice filled the air. "We have work to
do. No time for napping now."

Finn stared up out of the hole at the blue sky as the tree
branches swayed with more birds swooping in to join the
others. The clouds were forming soft plush animals, something
from his childhood as he sank further into the darkness
behind him.

Neil sat on the edge of the hole shaking his head. He was
always sitting on the edge of holes. "No time for drifting off. Get
your ass out of there."

"Give me a hand." Finn reached his arm up, but Neil didn't
extend his own. "You have to do this all yourself. You're a big

boy. Pull yourself up by your britches and get the hell out of there."

"It's kind of nice down here. It's cool and quiet," Finn said. "I just want to go back to sleep."

"Yeah, that's what she wants."

"Who wants?"

"Just open your eyes and look around. Listen to your little brother. Things might seem okay right now, but unless you stand up, they're going to get a lot worse."

Finn grumbled something under his breath. Something even he didn't understand and forced himself to open his eyes a little, just a crack. A different sort of light came through the haze. Something more shadowy and harsh.

Finn moaned. "Neil, I think I messed up."

"You sure as hell did mess up, but there's still time. So fight it."

"Fight it," Finn mumbled. His throat was sore and the pain in his head came surging back now, like rolling thunder across his consciousness. It clouded his thoughts. He winced and clenched his fists while opening his eyes a little further.

Neil moved off to the side of the hole and the walls of dirt and worms faded away and the stillness had all the same qualities of relaxing in bed or on a living room couch, but something wasn't right. The solitude encompassed him until another whoosh filled the air above him. The light became brighter, and he opened his eyes halfway, now peeking through a crack in the sky, but it wasn't the sky. He was peeking through his eyelids as a crack of blue and beige shadows transformed into a woman holding a muddy shovel.

Finn leaned forward as far as he could, but hit his forehead on something in the darkness. Lifting his aching arms, he felt a wooden wall above him. The rough edges of cheap wood splintered and snagged at his fingertips as he explored the barrier. Chunks of dirt slipped through the cracks in the wood and dropped onto his face.

He was inside a crate of some kind. A cage. A homemade casket.

Another whoosh above him, and the world faded a little more. Through the cracks he spotted Zelda above him throwing shovelfuls of dirt down over the cheap wooden box where he lay. He could see the dirt walls of the hole at the edge of his vision. He couldn't be more than three or four feet below the earth, but it was enough, wasn't it? Just deep enough to bury him... alive?

Panic set in as he sprang awake and pounded his fists on the inside of the crate. "No, Zelda, don't do this! You can't." But he was trapped. Trapped like Catherine's corpse jammed behind the wall in Emmie's basement, and the only difference was that Zelda hadn't severed *his* ring finger. "My lips are sealed..." he mumbled with the last bit of his humor as the irony of the horrific situation flooded in. Not that Zelda could have murdered Catherine, anyway. That was impossible, since she hadn't even been born yet. But...

Stop thinking and act. He screamed, "Get me out of here!"

Through the cracks in the cage, she seemed not to hear him, yet she recited odd sentences over and over that he recognized as voodoo. "... here lies his spirit. Take him still living, god of death, Maman Brigitte, and Erzulie... my gift to you. Thank you... let him sleep in your arms."

As she scooped up another shovelful of dirt from the pile next to her, Finn spotted a wheelbarrow next to the pile, and the memory of Zelda lifting him into it came back to him. *Stronger than she looks.* It was just a distant foggy memory, but it had jostled him awake enough to see the grass and forest ahead.

"I don't like to leave messes," she said without expression. "Mama always said clean up after yourself. So I better do what Mama says."

"No, you don't have to do what she says. Just let me out. I won't say a thing."

She ignored him and another shovelful of dirt slammed down on the crate, blocking most of the daylight streaming in through the cracks. Finn pushed with all his strength against the boards, searching for any flaws in its construction. One section of board was loose, and he pushed sideways, moving it half an inch out, but no farther than that. It stopped against the resistance of the dirt behind it. Another whoosh of dirt above him and all the light was gone.

Absolute darkness.

Finn's heartbeat pounded as he huffed in air.

No, slow yourself down, Finn. Don't panic. Think this through and you might make it. I will make it. I can't end like this. I can make it out if I just use my brain.

Finn screamed and pushed one last time all his strength against the lid above him. The wood crate wasn't strong, but it was strong enough, and he couldn't get any leverage while lying on his back.

Turn over.

Finn squirmed his way onto his side and forced the boards above him to give just a little, far enough so that he gained more leverage. The sound of dirt dropping above him faded with each whoosh. The sound of his breathing filled the air. His shoulders were uncomfortably angled in his new position, smashed up against the top and bottom of the crate as he forced himself to push out against the sides. The one place where he had loosened a board earlier wiggled a little more. He worked at the nail with everything he had, moving it back and forth slowly, then faster and faster, until it grew hot and snapped off. He yanked on it and pulled it in with him. Dirt flowed in along with it, followed by a twisted, snaking root. Pulling on the root, he used it for leverage to pull himself into a more comfortable position.

No time to get comfortable, Finn.

Grasping handfuls of dirt, he ran his fingers outside the crate along the sides as far as he could reach until his hand broke through into a pocket of air.

It was an open space within the dirt about the size of his own arm. A gopher hole?

Oh, that's good, a nice, convenient passage to lead the little critter straight to my body when I'm dead. Come and get me, boys. Supper's on!

Breaking through more dirt, he displaced another few handfuls to clear away a section along the side of the crate so that he made more room for himself to maneuver. Then, board by board, he loosened the nails from each one. He thought to use the nail clipper on his key chain. Maybe he could speed things up by using the nail file on it to cut through the nails. He checked his pocket. Empty. Of course, she had emptied his pockets before burying him. No sense in leaving him with a way out.

Something poked against his stomach while maneuvering to pull out another board. There was something with him in the crate, near his stomach. His fingers ran over the object and he formed a picture of what the item looked like in the darkness. A tiny figure like a doll. It was similar to the artifact he had found on the body in the basement of Emmie's house. Almost identical.

The image of the woman they'd found curled up in the hole filled his mind. *No, I won't end up like her.*

Finn increased his struggling to break through the side of the crate, clearing out inch after inch of space beside him and following the hole as it moved upward.

Please let it go all the way to the surface.

But it was only the size of his arm. He would need to widen it by scooping away the dirt with his palm. With nowhere else to put the dirt, he brought it inside the crate and pushed it down toward his feet.

How much oxygen do I have?

Don't think about it.

Pulling off another board, he used the loose plank instead of his palm to scoop away the dirt in onto his chest and then pushed it down in greater amounts near his feet, scooping and pushing, over and over. There seemed to be more dirt than there was open space as he continued.

What if the gopher hole is blocked?

He scooped again and dug further, ripping another board from the side of the crate. The dirt above him threatened to collapse as the hole widened. Maybe if he pulled too many boards away it would destabilize the structure. A collapse would end his escape and that would be it.

I've got no choice.

Slow and steady, Finn.

He slid himself up toward the hole a few inches and to the side. Pushing one arm into the hole as far up as he could, he discovered there was a little more space up further. Maybe just enough to get his chest through the opening and sit up. He had seen that the hole in which Zelda had put him wasn't more than a few feet. Just pushing through the opening a little further might get his head above the surface, if he was lucky.

Feeling lucky, Finn?

Not right now.

A patch of dirt and dust rained down as if something above the ground had dropped on him. Maybe just the earth settling, or maybe Zelda had danced on his grave after she'd finished. It was impossible to know if she was still up there waiting to make sure he didn't escape. The only sound was the thumping of his pulse in his ears and the shallow echo of each panicked breath.

A few more inches cleared away and his hopes rose. It might be enough space for him to escape. It will *have* to be enough.

He scooped faster, moving his arms mechanically, twisting a little further each time until he snaked forward far enough to poke his head out of the side of the crate. There was a little more space below the crate, a little pocket of air that he used to push the dirt from above back inside the crate.

It was a simple matter of displacing the dirt. Simple math.

Neil always said: Just use your brain, dummy.

The handfuls of dirt yielded more roots and several worms as he filled in the space near his feet, which allowed it to push forward, and he broke off two more boards so that his shoulders and head now stuck out of the side of the crate. A few more inches of open area above him, a few inches less below. He moved like a giant worm through the darkness.

Without the gopher hole, he was sure he wouldn't have made it that far. He would have suffocated by that time. But there was no guarantee that the hole ran unblocked to the surface.

He tried not to think about it. It was a race against time.

Just don't panic.

Filling in the crate behind him and digging out more dirt from the gopher hole, he rose more than a foot as his entire chest protruded from the crate. He had created a pocket of dirt just large enough for his body, but there was still no sign of the surface.

Using both hands, he dug faster now, pulling the dirt down over his chest and packing it into the crate, leaving the voodoo artifact behind.

Stretching his arms into the gopher hole above him, he found that it angled sideways. At least he hadn't run into the animal yet.

Now the trick was to get his legs underneath his body. Clearing away more space and clinging to several thick roots, he pulled himself up far enough to move his feet in under him. Gasping for breath, he sat in a squatted position with more dirt raining down on his face. The soil above him was more solid and full of roots.

I'm getting close to the surface.

If Zelda had only buried me a foot or two lower, I wouldn't have had a chance.

You're not out of the hole yet.

Finn pulled harder at the roots above him, letting the earth go down over his chest. A worm landed on his face, squirming over his cheek before falling away. Spitting the dirt from his mouth, he found it hard to breathe as he moved up into a space only large enough for his head.

Struggling to break through the tough soil, he hacked away as fast as he could. The air was running low, and he was feeling light-headed.

Not long now.

Then a sparkle of light filled his vision, blinding him for a moment as he gasped for joy. A sense of relief rushed over him, but he held back his excitement. She might still be up there. With the cool air rushing in, he took deep breaths and moved a little slower, trying to avoid creating a disturbance.

It felt like hours beneath the ground as he paused and let the panic subside. He listened for any sounds of Zelda, but continued gradually making the hole a little larger to allow more air to come in.

The fresh air was invigorating. He glanced up at the partly cloudy sky.

Things could be worse. At least it wasn't raining. I would have drowned.

As his mind cleared and he pushed a little higher, he poked his head out of the hole and looked around as much as he could. If Zelda was up there waiting for him, she would certainly have killed him as soon as he'd dared to escape.

A few inches higher, his muscles burned. Letting the dirt and hole grow slightly bigger just enough to give him space, air, and light, he rested and listened. Only the sweet sound of birds and tree leaves rustling in the branches overhead. He allowed the air to refresh his energy.

I almost died.

I almost became one of them.

Still no sign of Zelda, so he moved up further. His determination to stop her propelled him out of the hole, and he dropped to the grass, exhausted and filthy.

Thank God for gophers. He would never complain about them ever again.

Can't keep a good man down.

He didn't recognize anything around him, but he was alive.

"Now, where the hell am I?"

❧ 21 ❧

Finn trudged out of the forest to a road and tried to clean off the dirt as much as possible, although anyone driving by must have surely thought he was homeless. Coming out of the forest had been disconcerting as the countryside all looked the same, but luckily the sun was about to rise, and he caught his bearings by looking at the shadows. The road ran north-south, so if he was south of Summerton, then by going north he should run into the main highway running through town.

But there was no telling how far away Zelda had taken him. He could be hours away from Tommy's house, so he started walking north.

Stomping along to knock some of the mud away from his clothes and shoes, he was correct in assuming that nobody would stop and give him a ride. He didn't blame them. He certainly wouldn't have let anyone in his shape into his car.

After twenty minutes, he spotted a sign revealing he was on Highway 22. That had been the same road he'd used to get to Summerton. At least he was headed in the right direction.

All his muscles ached and his head still throbbed, but he trudged forward without stopping. A dry mouth was nothing compared to what he'd already endured, and he recognized some of the scenery from his drive earlier that day. Eventually, he would get there.

After walking for nearly two hours, he spotted the town ahead, and he considered stopping at each house along the way to ask for water, but he doubted anyone would open the door with dirt covering his clothes.

By then he wished the police would stop and pick him up, but he knew it wouldn't help beyond the brief break from thirst. If he talked about what happened without plausible evidence, it would only lead to them to think he was homeless or on drugs. Tommy's house was at the south edge of town, not far away, and if the police hadn't discovered Tommy yet, he could get inside and warn the girls about Zelda.

He touched his empty pocket instinctually, then cursed. He knew he didn't have his phone, but he would call them first thing at Tommy's. What was Emmie's phone number again? It was on his speed dial, but he could only remember the area code. 612. Sarah's number was also a blank.

Trudging to the top of a hill in the road, he spotted Tommy's driveway from a distance. Finn's car was missing. Zelda must have taken it. What else had she taken from the house? Would Tommy still be there? Had the police already stopped by? A thousand questions popped into his mind, but now seeing the house gave him a second wind.

Arriving at the driveway a short time later, he forced himself to keep moving forward to avoid collapsing. Walking to the front door, he spotted the doorbell camera and the camera over the garage door staring back at him. He remembered that Tommy had recorded everything, and he knew he could figure out, or the police could, where that information was kept. But following the cable down from the camera, he spotted the two severed ends of cable where someone had cut it.

His heart sank. If Zelda had cut that cable, then she had most likely cut the other cables too.

What if she's still here?

He couldn't shake that fear as he went to the front door and slinked cautiously inside, stepping softly over the creaking wooden floors in the entryway. His ears perked up and his skin crawled while listening for any signs that Zelda had anticipated his escape and was waiting for him just ahead, ready to finish him off.

Walking through the living room, there was no sign of her, and he calmed a bit. As his pulse slowed, the exhaustion of his escape set in. His stomach growled, although he wasn't hungry. But his throat was on fire, and if he didn't drink something soon he would faint from dehydration. Before going to the office, he stopped at the kitchen and drank three full glasses of water from the tap while keeping an eye out for anything that moved. He licked his lips after drinking the water, and the taste of dirt nauseated him.

Arriving at the office, he pushed the door open, and found Tommy's body in the same location, on the floor where he had fallen as Finn watched him cut his own throat at the hands of Zelda's magic. Tommy's skin was white, and his crumpled body lay serene, almost playful in his final pose within the pools of blood that had stained most of the floor. *Poor man.*

But Finn had to keep going; he had to get to the police with the evidence, or Tommy's death would be in vain. He stepped around the blood to where Tommy kept the tapes and followed a cable along the wall across the room to a closet door. Zelda could have cut that cable too, but if it had recorded her up until that moment... He opened the door and spotted some disconnected wires dangling beside an empty space on a shelf where the surveillance recorder must have been. It was gone.

"Dammit!"

He looked around for his phone and wallet, or anything else that might allow him to get help, but the desk was a mess. Pushing some papers aside, he realized his laptop had gotten buried beneath the clutter. He had knocked over some folders while moving around during Tommy's horrifying struggle. And when Zelda pulled out the external hard drive to strike him with it, she must not have seen it.

Not so tidy for a slick murderer, are you?

His head throbbed as he opened the laptop and logged in. The camera's software was prompting him for a location to save his recording.

Had it recorded any of the attack?

He carefully saved the recording to a folder on his desktop, then tensed as he watched the video.

The murder was there. Not the best angle, but it had recorded enough. Zelda's face was clear, and the feed showed both Finn and Tommy. It showed her dragging Finn across the room after knocking him out. She had brought in a wheelbarrow through the back door and had used it to move him outside, leaving Tommy dead where he lay.

Finn's stomach churned as he finished the video, but he saved it to the flash drive, the same one Tommy had given him containing some of his surveillance videos from the murder of his daughter, and removed it from the laptop before slipping it into his pocket.

Now if he could get to the police without more interference from Zelda.

He paused beside Tommy before he stepped away, careful not to disturb any evidence. "Tommy, I won't forget you. And I won't let you or your daughter down. We've got her. You were right, and without your videos, Zelda might have gotten away again."

Grabbing the bedsheet that Tommy had used to prevent them from seeing the corkboard on their first visit, he gently laid it over Tommy.

On his way out, Finn cleaned his face as much as possible at the sink in the bathroom. Seeing the bruises in the mirror where Zelda had struck him, he cringed, and they throbbed even more as he tried to nurse them. He also noticed several bloody cuts around his cheeks and forehead. The police would look at him side-eyed because of his clothes, but wiping off his face would help. He also grabbed a bottle of water and an apple from the fridge. It was going to be a long day.

Outside, Tommy's car was in the driveway, but after a short search, he couldn't find the keys and thought the police might consider it auto theft, so he decided to walk instead. The center of town wasn't more than a mile away, although it would feel like a thousand miles in his condition.

The walk to the police station took every ounce of strength out of him, and he could not help but feel triumphant as he walked through the door, approached the nearest officer and held up the flash drive.

"I want to report a murder. Actually, several."

❧ 22 ❧

Zelda...

Emmie must have heard Finn repeat the woman's name hundreds of times in the past forty-eight hours, ever since Emmie and Sarah had gone to get him from the Lake Ridge Hospital's Emergency Room, the same hospital where Sarah worked, and where they'd treated him for a head wound, dehydration and fatigue.

They'd taken him home to Caine House, and had stayed with him, although he could get around without assistance. In bits and pieces, and often out of order, he'd told them the tale of discovering the surprising identity of the serial killer of four young women; then of Tommy's death, Zelda's attack, and her attempt to bury him alive.

Seeing him in the hospital bed on the morning of October fifth, with bandages covering the left side of his head, had been horrifying. They'd feared the worst, until his smug smirk convinced them he wasn't suffering from any other delusions, apart from the usual one of thinking he was infallible.

After talking with the hospital staff in charge of him, Sarah had led Emmie out of his room as he lay in a blue hospital gown above the bed's thin white sheets, the vein in his arm still connected to an IV line. She'd gone into nurse mode, speaking straight to the point, yet full of heart. "He doesn't have a concussion, and his vitals are good. But getting buried alive, most people fear that the most. The trauma might not start now. We have to stay with him and make sure he's all right."

Finn's trauma hadn't even shown during the Lunar Stillness, which had come and gone the night before without drama. They had braced for the worst and had huddled around Finn's bed, with the women clutching their protection dolls and Finn a bottle of rum that Sarah strongly urged him not to drink. But nothing at all had happened, to their relief.

And the news, both on television and online, told of no murders even remotely similar to what had happened to Natalie and the others.

So on the morning of October seventh, forty-eight hours after Finn's ordeal, Emmie looked at him with a broad smile. He was lying on the couch with a green and white quilt covering him, while the sun streamed in through an unshaded window across the room and lit the area over his feet and legs. He looked like an old man, with his messy hair and unshaven face, and he kept his eyes closed while pulling the quilt up to his chin as if he couldn't get enough of it.

Sarah had left for work in the early hours of the morning, but had promised to come home early to help care for Finn, so it was just the two of them until she returned. But there were plenty of things to read, and Betty's house was a short walk away.

Still, Emmie wanted to wake him, if for no other reason than to talk to someone. Sarah *had* mentioned he wasn't supposed to sleep too much because of the head wounds. She cleared her throat and pushed the guilt aside. "How did you sleep after we left?"

He shuddered, which made her jump; but then he grinned and straightened the back of his hair with his fingers. "Well, with the help of my friend called rum."

At least the trauma hadn't killed Finn's sense of humor. "You kept drinking? Should you have, considering?"

He gestured to the pwen doll that was propped up on the table next to a book of Betty's that Emmie had been reading before he came down. On voodoo, of course, though she was sick of the subject.

"Should you be keeping a voodoo doll, considering?"

She stared at the doll, wondering if he was forgetting things because of the head wound. "I told you, the high priestess of the Arcane group gave it to me the other day. It's supposed to protect us from evil spirits."

"So they saved us?"

"Yeah, what if they worked?"

"Right," he said. "Or maybe, who the hell knows?"

"I'm trying to find out more info about it. Can you send me the picture of that doll we found with Catherine's body?"

"Zelda took my phone."

That name again. Hearing the woman's name sent a renewed chill through Emmie. They gazed into each other's eyes for a moment, and his expression mirrored her own fear. Zelda was still out there.

Emmie nodded. "You'll get it back."

"Not anytime soon. The police took my laptop too, for evidence. I'm useless."

"Hardly."

He groaned and repositioned himself, but didn't sit up. "This moon thing, that's what drove a woman to kill several others?"

They had told Finn about what they'd discovered in the Arcane Temple and about the High Priestess Char Goodman, and how they'd come to the same conclusion as him: that another murder was about to happen. They had told him about the significance of the ten years and all the rest. But he kept bringing it up, as if endlessly turning it over in his mind, and she couldn't blame him, as Zelda had almost finished him off as well, and in the most horrible of ways. Buried alive.

"The moon does drive people insane, they say," he added casually. "And Zelda sure as hell was a nutcase. But the blood and all that, the ring finger. Renewal, you said? Wasn't working for her." His eyes seemed to glisten, or was it the light, and he shook his head. "For that she killed four young women with lives ahead of them, and a standup guy like Tommy. That crazy..."

Without finishing the insult, he turned his face to catch the sun that had crept up across his chest, and Emmie noticed an odd angle to a chunk of his hair at the back of his head: a section jutted straight out. "Turn around."

Finn gave her a strange look. "What?"

She held out her hand toward his hair. "Turn to the side. Hadn't noticed that before. A chunk of your hair is missing."

"Damn." He stroked the back of his head.

A flash of fear passed over his face, but his expression soon changed to anger. "I must have ripped it out climbing from the grave."

"It'll grow back," she said.

"Come on. Find it in the book and tell me what to expect. Better that you give me the bad news now."

Emmie sighed and turned pages until she located a passage and started reading out loud. *"The materials used to create a pwen doll usually consist of items connected with the target, and its purpose, whether good or malicious. Its color is important, as a dark color can signify death or sickness, while a light color can signify life or health. The stuffing can be made from cotton, cloth, or other soft substances, which can also affect its purpose. It can be filled with feathers and sand for protection or bones and hair of the person to be held captive."* Emmie gestured to her white pwen doll. "Looks like I've got a good one. On the outside, anyway."

Finn rose in his pajamas from the couch and moved slowly to the table, then picked up Emmie's pwen doll and squished it. "This one feels different from the one I found with me in the coffin, which must be where my good haircut went. There's something sharp inside of this, I'm sure. I can feel something poking through the cloth."

"Let me take a look." Emmie squeezed it. Finn was correct, but she hadn't noticed it before.

"Mine must have had the hair that's gone from my head," he said a little grimly. "And the mouth, I think, was sewn. But I guess I didn't die, so they couldn't keep me quiet."

"Why didn't she drain your blood, do you think?"

"She discovered she couldn't control me through voodoo because I fought back. She could have cut my throat, though, and she didn't. When she was... burying me, she did say that she was offering up a live victim to one of her gods. That they had told her to do that. The purpose of killing the women must have been different. She didn't mean to use me or Tommy for the Lunar Stillness thing, she just wanted to silence us because we knew what she had done."

Finn picked up Emmie's doll again and carried it to the kitchen. A few minutes later, he came back with the doll in one hand and a small piece of something in his other palm facing up. "Look at this."

"You cut it open?"

"Just a little, to get a better look inside." It was a piece of a shredded black feather. "So, what's the significance of that?"

"Black is the opposite of what you'd think. It's for protection, just like the feathers, as they said."

"Yes, but whoever created mine, and Natalie's, and Catherine's, all had the same intention. Control on a deep level, following the victim after death. Nobody would bother with creating a doll like this without a seriously messed up purpose."

Emmie stared at the doll in Finn's hand. "When we went to find Natalie's spirit, it seemed like she wanted to communicate, but she couldn't. Something else, a more aggressive spirit, got in the way."

"We freed Catherine from the hole," Finn said, "yet you say she can't speak? Her mouth is still sewn shut?"

"Because she's still attached to the doll somehow." Emmie nodded, thinking. "Zelda must be very skilled at this stuff. She must have learned it from someone. Who?"

"Maybe someone in the voodoo group now? This dark group Tommy hinted at. Makes sense. Every cult or philosophy has its dark side, right?"

The doorbell rang. They jumped a little. After all, Zelda was still on the loose.

Finn set the doll down on the coffee table and headed toward the door, moving at a slower pace than usual, but better than before.

Emmie followed him. "Be careful. Sarah wouldn't use the doorbell."

"Would Zelda?" Finn opened the door.

A man in a black police detective uniform stood in the door with a slight grin. His badge read, "Murray."

Finn stepped forward and shook the man's hand. "Detective Murray. What brings you out here?"

"Thought I'd give you the news in person. We've arrested Zelda Hyde."

❧ 23 ❧

Emmie surged with joy, but Finn was wobbling, and she grabbed his arm, thinking he might fall back.

Finn let out a loud sigh. "Thank God."

His arm trembled within her grasp. Maybe it was just his body still recovering from the ordeal, but it was obvious it had impacted him more deeply than she'd imagined.

But a moment later, he gently pulled his arm away and turned to Emmie while gesturing at the man. "He helped me at the police station, and we had a long chat about you-know-who at the hospital, after they'd patched me up, and before you arrived."

Finn invited Detective Murray to come in and directed him to a different room from the one with all the voodoo books and the doll. "Where did you catch her?"

"At the University of Minnesota campus, someone reported a suicidal woman near a sorority house and the local police captured Ms. Hyde around there, wearing the same flowery raincoat shown in the video you provided. She's being held at the Minneapolis Police Department now."

Finn swallowed. "She must have truly lost it, then?"

"Apparently, she kept screaming she was fed up, fed up, fed up. It's what she is still saying, keeps repeating it."

"Oh, well!" Finn exclaimed in high irony. "Having to hack and murder multiple people does that to a girl. Just makes her truly rethink her career choice." He calmed down a little after the detective threw him a strange look, then added more soberly, "What happens now?"

"We'll keep in touch. I just stopped by to give you the news, and also to let you know that your car was recovered from a forest outside Summerton. It's at the Minneapolis Police Department now."

"That helps if it's in one piece. What about my phone? And laptop?"

The detective shook his head. "No phone. And can't give back your laptop, yet. Sorry."

"The weird stuff in it," Finn blurted out. "Just remember, I'm a journalist and also researching a novel. About, uh, ghosts."

"We won't look at the weird stuff without your permission. Or a warrant."

Finn pursed his lips but said nothing.

"What if she gets out on bail?" Emmie asked.

"The odds of the judge releasing her are slim, considering the charges. We'll interrogate her again when I get back. A lot of people just confess when we show them the evidence we have. We hope to get a swift resolution."

"But if she acts looney, her lawyers could throw any confession out," Finn pointed out. "She *needs* to be in jail."

Detective Murray held up his palms in a pacifying gesture. "Or in an asylum. We put the evidence of those murders and what we found since then in front of a judge, and I doubt she will be on the street again, even with a team of crack lawyers, which she probably doesn't have the money to pay for."

"Her mother might," Finn said slowly.

"We've spoken to the old lady. She is shocked and disgusted beyond belief and doesn't seem to be too in love with her daughter. Acts as if she suspected something was wrong with her all along but couldn't tell what. Zelda's daughter is still in Los Angeles, making plans to return because of her mother's arrest."

"Poor Grace." Emmie stared at the floor.

Finn scratched the back of his head, brushing his fingers against his poorly cut hair. "Let me ask you something. Is it possible to sit in the interrogation room with you or let me ask her some questions?"

"What sort of questions?"

"I have to know why she did this."

Detective Murray smiled and inched back in the chair. "I'm sure all that will come out in the investigation. I'll keep you updated."

Finn leaned toward him. There was intelligence and warmth behind Detective Murray's eyes. It was clear Finn *wanted* to believe the detective, but also remembered what Tommy Cooper had said about the investigation into Natalie's murder. The lack of progress, of tying things together fast enough. Finn wasn't going to trust that everything would turn out all right.

"I think I can help in this case. Zelda is obviously a little *off*, as you can tell by her behavior. She's involved with voodoo." With a canny look, Finn added, "She believes the mumbo jumbo is real. But I think I can help you get some answers. Let me talk to her for ten minutes. It can't hurt, right? I'm in journalism, remember? I'm used to getting people to talk, and I bet you'll be surprised at what I can dig up."

"*That* might be a confession that gets thrown out by lawyers," Detective Murray said.

"Not if you are right there. I will just be a victim, asking why she would do that to me, boohoo and boohoo. If I'm right, she wants to talk, but to me. Every criminal is vain, and I am the one who found her out with Tommy. She will want to show off, prove that I don't know anything. Trust me."

"Sounds like you've done something like it before." The detective pondered it for a moment. "Tell you what, I'll go back and speak to the lieutenant and give you a call if he is all right with it. Sound good?"

"Agreed, except, I don't have a phone."

The detective nodded knowingly. "Good point."

Emmie gave him her phone number, and they walked with him to the door. After shaking hands again, he headed out to his car just as Sarah pulled into the driveway.

They waited at the door until the detective had left and Sarah came inside. She still wore her scrubs, and the smell of antiseptic hung in the air around her. It made Finn's nostrils flare, and she seemed to pick up on his reaction.

"Does it bother you? The smell?" She touched his arm.

He shrugged. "It'll... take time."

She gestured to the driveway with a worried look. "Is everything okay?"

Finn and Emmie took turns filling Sarah in on the news of the arrest and Finn's plans to confront Zelda.

"Just... be careful, Finn," Sarah said, not hiding the deep concern on her face.

He looked into her eyes, then turned back toward the couch in the living room. "I'm a lot better now."

Sarah went upstairs to shower and change, her familiar routine after working at the hospital, and Emmie joined her a little later in her room where they could talk alone. "We'll have to watch him."

Sarah brushed her wet hair. The purple was only in the ends now. "I think he'll hold up."

"I'm just worried that things might... fall apart. I wouldn't want Finn battling the police for years like Tommy did." Emmie met Sarah's gaze. "But this isn't like that this time, is it? They got her, and she'll never get out."

Sarah shook her head. "She won't."

Emmie nodded slowly and sat on Sarah's bed. "And I don't know about you, but I can't get Alice out of my mind. We came here for that, and we are far from finding out how she died and how Catherine died. We swore to help her move on, and we haven't done that yet. So... I know it's so soon after so much craziness, but what do you say we go back to Hyde House today? With Zelda gone, it'll be a lot easier to check out those graves in the backyard, and we don't know how long it will be before Veronica comes back from LA. I hate to take advantage of Grace being there alone with the nurse, but it's the only time we will have to go back and try to communicate again with Daniel."

Sarah smiled and stared into her eyes. "You had me at 'back to Hyde House.' What, I'm not allowed to be brave?"

They headed downstairs a little later and told Finn what they planned to do. Sitting up on the couch now with the quilt over his lap, he agreed it was a low-risk opportunity to get some answers.

Emmie received a text message in the middle of their conversation. *Detective Murray here. Finn can meet with Zelda at 4pm today at the Minneapolis 6th Precinct. Can he make it?* Emmie shared the message with Finn.

He stood up and scowled, tossing the quilt to the side. "Hell yeah!" A moment later, he winced and sat back down.

"I don't think you're ready." Sarah sat next to him and returned to nurse mode while she inspected Finn's head wound, noting that it would take some time to heal. "Just take it easy. You don't have to do this."

"I do."

Emmie and Sarah looked at each other. It was obvious they were thinking the same thing. Nothing they could say would change his mind.

When three p.m. rolled around, Finn came down from upstairs, neatly dressed and with gel over the back of his hair.

"I was thinking," he said. "Stay out of sight around Hyde House, even though it's safe without Zelda around. It probably traumatized the old woman too. Actually, I don't like the idea of you gals going there without me."

"Thanks for the mansprotecting," Emmie said. "But we aren't like you and won't do anything stup—*daring*."

He narrowed his eyes at her, and she quickly went on.

"And don't you provoke the serial killer too much. We don't know whether the voodoo gives her special powers and she could choke you from a distance."

Finn smirked and pulled at a leather string around his neck until a little figurine emerged from under his sweater. "Just in case, I have this powerful protection amulet you gave me. I like Betty's stuff a lot better than the hairy voodoo stuff, so thanks."

As they moved outside, he added, "And when have I ever pushed things? I intend to get answers out of Zelda today, despite the fact that I'm scared." Finn swallowed. "There, I said it. I'm scared, but maybe I'm the only one who can drag the truth out of her, because I've seen what she can do firsthand. The cops don't understand her like I do. This woman is really messed up. I could tell that while she attacked me and Tommy, but I won't let this go until I get answers."

Sarah nodded slowly. "Call us when you're finished. Don't keep us hanging."

Finn touched his pocket. "I don't have a phone, remember? But after the meeting, I'll drive to Minneapolis and pick up a new one."

Sarah pulled the phone from her pocket and held it out to him. "You can borrow mine, if you want, just in case you have an emergency."

He pushed it back and cupped her hands over the phone with a wink. "You worry too much, and you might need it."

She grinned but didn't pull away. "You never miss an opportunity to flirt, do you?"

Finn laughed. "Never. Especially as it helps take away my headache."

"Glad to help."

"Remember to call us as soon as you get your new phone, so we know you're okay."

A puzzled look passed over Finn's face. "You know, I can't call you, as I realized when I almost died. I don't know your phone numbers."

"I'll write them down," Sarah said, running back inside. Within a minute, she returned and passed him the numbers. Finn slipped the paper into his pocket.

Sarah stepped up a few stairs, then glanced back. "And after you're all done," she said, "if you feel better, come back to our place and I'll put some new bandages on those wounds. You've got a nurse here, you might as well take advantage of me."

"You're phrasing it like that because you think I'm weak."

"I've had to deal with plenty of difficult patients." Sarah continued up the steps. "I could kick your ass anytime."

"Fair enough. We'll put that to the test." Finn turned to Emmie and winced while leaning back with his hands on his hips. "Not really, though. Damn, my whole body hurts. I feel like I just dug myself out of a grave and walked a few miles."

"Now you're just trying to elicit sympathy."

"Wrong audience?"

With a sarcastic smile, she tilted her head at him. "See how you do with Zelda."

Touching the amulet as if to make sure it was there, he widened his eyes and got into his car. Emmie returned to the house laughing. With a little god of whatsit protecting him, what could go wrong?

🐾 24 🐾

The sun was still up by the time Emmie and Sarah stood before Hyde House for the second time, but they wouldn't have much time before it dropped below the horizon. The windows of the house stared back at them, giving nothing away.

"So, how are we going to do this?" Sarah asked.

"We can't just go knocking on her door. Not after what happened to Zelda. It didn't sound as if it had exactly devastated Grace, but it *was* our friend who got her daughter arrested."

Sarah gestured to the white sedan in the driveway. "There's a hospital parking sticker on the back window of that car. The nurse, Donna, must be in there with Grace. As we thought, she's not alone."

"She'll be busy with an old woman who can't really move. Veronica isn't here, which is what makes me think we can try this. If the nurse comes out before we're done, we'll just act innocent. That we came to see how she was after the news. How's that?"

"Sounds as good as it'll get."

"I can't imagine what it must be like to find out your daughter killed a bunch of people, no matter what she said to the police."

"Could have been the shock talking. Didn't look like there was a great love there, but it's still heartbreaking."

"We'll just make a quick detour to the graves in the backyard. I hope Daniel is there this time or I'm not sure how we'll get answers."

Emmie suggested they turn off their phones too. Even with the sound and vibration off, the screen could light up at a message or call, and they wouldn't have time to fiddle with the settings. She kept her eyes on the front door as they passed around the left side of the house to the back toward the garage. The blinds over all the windows were pulled down, so that would reduce the chance that anyone inside would see them.

Entering the backyard, they passed the garage and the wall of pine trees beyond that until Emmie spotted the flower garden Grace had talked about. Even from across the lawn, it was impressive. Rows and rows of different flower types spread out in every direction.

Emmie whispered. "How do they take care of all this?"

"If Zelda did before, this will all die now. Or Donna will have to do it."

"Let me know if you feel anything. We need to try hard to see Daniel this time."

"You felt him before. He's got to be around here somewhere."

They stepped over to the garden. The magnitude of the work someone had done in the garden became clearer up close. Not just a simple flower garden, this was a sanctuary with a stone bench near the center and a path leading through the maze of roses, dahlias, orchids, and several other varieties that surrounded two small gravestones at the center beside the bench. Everything was neatly manicured and packed into a circular parcel of land twenty or thirty feet wide. Beyond the garden was a wall of shrubs, set back as if designed to protect the garden from the weather and intruders.

"This is like a shrine to Daniel and Ruth." Emmie stepped

over to the bench and sat down. "Grace must pay a landscaper to take care of everything outdoors. I can't see Zelda having done *everything*."

Sarah joined her. "It's beautiful."

Emmie closed her eyes and sniffed the air. The aroma was like heaven. "No wonder she wanted us to see it."

Simple stone slabs marked the two graves that sat side-by-side.

∾

1896 - 1934 Daniel Hyde
1890 - 1976 Ruth Hyde

∾

EMMIE GLANCED AROUND THE AREA. NO SIGN OF DANIEL'S spirit, and a sinking sensation filled her chest. If this is where Daniel had killed himself, he should be there.

Emmie read the names on the gravestones again. Daniel Hyde, Loving Father. Ruth Hyde, Beloved Mother.

"I see now why Grace still lives here," Sarah said. "So much family history. I wonder what would happen to a gravesite like this if they sold the house. Doubt anyone else would keep it, and it would be up to the Hyde family to move the remains."

"But it's so strange." Emmie strained and focused on any spirits in the area. "I don't see him. Maybe my powers are fading."

When Emmie opened her eyes again, Sarah was watching her. "Anything?"

Emmie shook her head. "Nothing."

"I don't feel anything either. This can't be the place where he died. Maybe in the house?"

Emmie stared at the back side of the house. One window upstairs was uncovered. "I guess we don't know exactly where he killed himself. We'll need to get in there and take another look around."

"That won't be easy."

Emmie sighed. "Agreed." She looked at the roses. "Could something be blocking our psychic senses? If Daniel's spirit is in the house..." Emmie's gaze locked on to the upstairs bedroom window, the one window without a blind covering it. A man's expressionless face peered down at her. His pale, gaunt face sent a chill up her spine and she recognized him from the pictures on the walls of Grace's home.

Daniel.

✣ 25 ✣

It surprised Finn that he wasn't more nervous as he waited outside Zelda's interrogation room. Detective Murray's lieutenant had forced him to sign a waiver relinquishing his right to sue them in case things got "out of hand," but it didn't matter. He just wanted to get in there and see her expression when she realized she'd failed.

"Don't be confrontational," Detective Murray was telling him, "just get her talking and we'll use her own words against her later to get a confession."

"I understand."

"If she becomes hostile for any reason, stand up, step back, and I'll take care of it. Under no circumstances should you engage physically with the suspect. Is that understood?"

"Yes."

"She hasn't called a lawyer at this point, so your presence might evoke some information we can use to prosecute her. But you can't put words in her mouth, or a confession might be thrown out later."

Finn nodded. "Got it."

An officer standing at the door patted Finn down for the second time. He didn't blame them for their extreme security measures; a high-profile murder suspect in a gruesome string of murders like Zelda would make national news and they didn't want him to mess things up. Detective Murray nodded once to the officer standing at the door. The officer opened it, and Finn followed the detective into the interrogation room.

When Finn walked in, he met Zelda's eyes. Her expression changed from disgust to shock.

"You! *How?*"

She stood up and threw her arms on the table as if she would jump up and strangle him, but chains connected to her handcuffs held her back. The veins in her neck bulged, and she bared her teeth like a snarling wild dog. Her orange jumpsuit didn't hide her meaty hands and muscular arms, something Finn hadn't noticed during the visit to the house earlier.

Finn swallowed. Good thing they bolted the metal table to the ground.

Detective Murray stepped to his chair and motioned for Finn to pass behind him and take his seat.

Within a short time, Zelda's expression changed from rage to anger, then to annoyance, then to a phony grin, as if it didn't bother her at all that Finn had escaped from her inescapable nightmare.

Finn sat next to Detective Murray, directly across from Zelda, and neither of them looked away.

"Why is he here?" Zelda asked the detective. "You said it was someone *important to my case*."

"I didn't exactly say that. But who did you think I meant?" Detective Murray asked.

"Anyone but him," Zelda grumbled.

"So you know Mr. Adams?"

"I know what I know..." she chanted under her breath.

The detective's voice was gentle and soothing, like an adult talking to a child, and Zelda calmed a little more with each word he spoke. "Why were you so angry at this man?" He gestured to

Finn. "He's kind of snooty, true, but I think you only met him once, is that right?"

"Once too many."

"It's just odd seeing such a strong reaction from you when he walked into the room."

"I don't care about him."

"All right, but I think Mr. Adams just wants to know why you attacked him and Tommy Cooper two nights ago. He just wants to understand what he did to make you mad. That's all."

"I didn't touch either of them."

"At first, no, but you did see the video to the end, didn't you?"

Zelda lowered her gaze for a moment. "Yes."

"That was you, right?"

"The video showed I didn't kill anyone," she said slowly, as if she had said it before; as if now the detective was the child and she was the adult.

He nodded. "But it shows you attacked this man as he struggled to get away. You put him in a wheelbarrow. Where did you take him?"

"Dragged him out of the way."

"Why?"

"Take out the trash."

"Really? Is that your opinion of him?"

"Yes. Mama says to always clean up my messes."

Finn's breath stopped for a moment at hearing her words. He remembered them now. He sat upright. "That's what you said at the gravesite where you buried me."

The detective looked at Zelda. "Is that true?"

She grinned subtly. "The boy's got good hearing."

"Why go to so much trouble to get rid of him? Wouldn't it have been easier to leave him at the house?"

"He wouldn't *leave me alone*. Better to put him away somewhere where no one would ever find him. He wasn't supposed to be there, anyway." Zelda clutched her hair and pulled. "He might attract the wrong kind of attention."

"What's the wrong kind of attention?" Detective Murray asked.

"He's not just snooty. He's a pest. A cockroach. And those others too."

Finn shivered. *The girls.* "You wanted to hurt Emmie and Sarah too?"

"Do you think I'm stupid? You all came bearing gifts, but you had questions. I was watching you." She narrowed her eyes. "Curious eyes, wanting to look at everything. Pretending the questions were casual but asking a bunch." She scoffed at Finn, her chin meeting her chest and making her face longer, more of a rectangle than a square now. Her eyes were full of everything bad: malice, resentment, anger, madness, disdain.

Detective Murray spoke up. "So you didn't want people connecting his death with Tommy's death. Is that right?"

"No loose ends."

Opening a file, Detective Murray rifled through the autopsy photos of the four women Zelda had probably killed. Finn caught a glimpse of them, lying on gurneys in four different decades, pale with blue or purple lips and the same hole in their neck, and his stomach churned.

The detective tapped his finger on the photos. "That man you left bleeding on the floor was trying to find out what had happened to these women." He tapped Natalie's photo. "This was his daughter. Her name was Natalie."

Natalie's white skin clung to her bones as if she were an old woman. A close-up photo showed where her ring finger was missing.

"She was used for parts..." Finn mumbled.

Zelda cackled, and she put her hand over her mouth. Her beady eyes were almost shut in glee. She was beyond care, and the look of disdain she threw at Detective Murray showed it. "You want me to feel sorry for the girls and the fathers and mothers and all that, but he knows." She nodded at Finn. "They were used for parts. They didn't matter. The world is full of people. They come and go and don't know how to stay, so they don't matter."

"So you admit you killed them," Detective Murray asked softly. "For their... parts."

"I did what I had to do."

"Why did you have to do it?" Finn asked suddenly.

Zelda had turned away, as if the two men no longer interested her, but now she turned to Finn. "I'm good at it."

The detective sat back in his chair and rubbed his chin.

She narrowed her eyes at Finn and he leaned forward.

"What was that thing you placed with me in my grave?" he asked. "You said I was a gift to the gods. The doll too?"

Zelda's face lit up as if remembering a funny moment in her life. "It only works if you die. What a shame."

"What was it supposed to do?" Finn asked.

Zelda's eyes narrowed further. "I think you know."

Finn sat back in his chair and spoke without expression. "Silence me."

"Bingo."

Detective Murray didn't react, although he probably knew they'd gone into "mumbo-jumbo territory."

Finn forced an expression of confused admiration to bring out the "pest" in him. "It was as if... as if you knew a lot. About the gods. Where did you learn that? It wasn't at the temple, I bet."

Zelda and Finn locked gazes again; the detective had receded to the background. "Them?" Zelda lightly chuckled. "Don't insult me. I've never had anything to do with them. Waste of time."

"Why is that? Because you know what you're doing and they don't?" Finn glanced down at the photos of the dead women. "I can see that. Where did you learn all this?"

"I'm a natural," she boasted with a smug smile. "Everyone knows it."

"Who is everyone?" Finn asked quietly, careful not to move or

he might break the spell he had woven on her. The spell of vanity. "Who trusts you to be so good?"

"She trusts me to keep her healthy and happy." Tears glistened in her narrow monster eyes. Tears of pride? "Mama does."

In an instant, the room receded as if the walls had flown away and a vast emptiness surrounded him. It was just Zelda and him. Her teary eyes glistening while he gasped in a breath. There was no sound except his pulse pounding in his ears.

He pushed against the table and stood on shaking legs. *Mama*.

"What's wrong?" Detective Murray asked him.

He'd been told not to move suddenly, but that didn't matter anymore as he raced to the door. It wouldn't open. He slapped his palm against the cool metal surface. "Let me out. I need to leave *now*."

Glancing back, he saw Zelda was smiling like a little girl who had completed all her tasks and deserved a little gold star.

26

"It's him!" Emmie pointed to the window. "I saw his face."

"I see a dark silhouette," Sarah said.

Emmie focused on Daniel at that moment and tried to pull him from the house. If she could get him outside, they could have the conversation she needed. Staring at him through half-closed eyes, she pulled, but there was resistance in his spirit. Something was holding him back. She strained and watched for any reaction from him, but it made no difference. "I can't communicate with him."

Daniel moved back into the darkness.

Stepping toward the house, they found a back porch directly in front of them; it was the only way in if they planned a stealthy entrance.

Emmie glanced up at the unshaded window again. "Maybe he was up there all the time we were in the house the first time. It's strange that we didn't sense him."

"I still don't," Sarah said.

Too late to hide their presence. Emmie knocked. "When the nurse answers the door, you distract her while I go explore the upstairs bedrooms. It shouldn't take long."

"All right."

After a few moments, she knocked again a little more force-fully. The back door creaked open and stayed ajar like a gaping mouth. Nobody was there to greet them, either living or dead.

"Daniel?" Emmie whispered. "Is that you?"

No answer and no activity inside the house from what she could see.

"It must be him," Sarah said.

But neither of them stepped through the doorway. "I don't count that as a valid invitation," Emmie said.

"Well, we aren't vampires," Sarah reasoned. "We don't need one."

A man's voice came from deep inside the house. Not a menacing cry for help, but soft-spoken words. Inviting words.

"Daniel?" Emmie called.

The man's voice grew louder, yet Emmie still couldn't discern what he was saying. But with the door wide open, Emmie stepped into the doorway. "Daniel? If you can hear me, please come outside. We'd like to talk."

"Maybe they're all upstairs," Sarah said.

Emmie nodded. "Her bedroom is probably up there, not on the main floor. If we can just get Daniel down here..."

The man whispered again, this time a little more harshly. Still no sign of Grace or the nurse.

They avoided touching the door as it shifted while still propped open by an unseen force.

Emmie stepped in first, moving cautiously with each step to avoid unwanted noise. Not an ideal situation, but Daniel must be holding the door open for them.

An odd room came first. A sunroom full of flowers and plants, a bright, happy scene anyone would be proud to own. Grace obviously had a passion for everything flora.

"What was the nurse's name?" Emmie asked.

"Donna."

Emmie stood straight as they moved along, expecting to meet Donna at any moment. It would look better if they weren't discovered hunched forward like a burglar. Sarah did the same, seemingly understanding her intention.

They stepped down the main hallway leading to the front area, passing through the kitchen and dining room. All the lights were on, although the stillness and silence were awkward.

"Maybe she's taking a nap?" Sarah whispered.

"That makes sense."

Passing a separate study room, plenty of closets, and a wall of built-in shelves, they came to a closed door. Carefully cracking it open, Emmie found a stairway leading upstairs.

No need to say anything. Sarah nodded. They started up the stairs, taking special care to shift their weight as slowly as possible to avoid the creaking boards.

They heard no voices; Daniel had gone quiet, but they continued to the top of the stairs and turned down a winding hallway back to the room where Emmie had seen Daniel at the window.

Several framed portraits hung along the walls of the hallway, and they took a moment to glance at each of them. One of them showed Ruth and Daniel Hyde dressed up, standing in front of the house, and their faces beamed. A happy couple.

The doors to most other rooms were closed, except for the bathroom. Passing near one of them, Emmie thought she heard the sound of someone breathing. Maybe Grace and the nurse were inside. Probably sleeping, by the sound of it.

Following the hallway back to the room where she thought Daniel might have been, Emmie opened the door and stopped breathing. Plastic tarps covered the floor and in the center lay a woman's body in a pool of blood. Her skin was white and shriveled and her ring finger was gone, blood still draining from the ghastly wound.

Sarah gasped.

It was Donna.

27

"What's wrong?" Detective Murray asked Finn.

Finn's heart was beating faster every second. He just needed to get out and back to the girls. At least Detective Murray had let him out of the interrogation room, where Zelda seemed to be gloating. But she couldn't know where Emmie and Sarah had gone... Could she?

The detective stood in Finn's way. "What's all this about?"

For a moment, Finn considered telling him the truth, and maybe even asking for help, but how could he possibly explain everything? This wasn't something Detective Murray would understand, and there was no guarantee he would even go with him to Hyde House as fast as Finn needed to, even if Finn pleaded that his friends were in danger.

What sort of danger are we talking about? the detective would ask.

Voodoo, occult, magic.

There was no point in explaining anything. They had Zelda in custody. The serial murderer wouldn't escape, and the real-life, non-magic game was over. For him to even suggest they apprehend another person without evidence, especially an old, feeble woman, would just weaken the case against Zelda.

Grace. It was all about Grace.

Mama taught me to clean up after myself. Zelda's words swam through his mind, circling back to his consciousness every few seconds to spark a fresh jolt of panic.

"Mr. Adams?" the detective said. "Are you all right?"

"I'm fine." Finn grabbed his jacket from a coat rack nearby and, out of habit, ran his fingers over his pocket as he put it on. *Dammit, no phone.* "Can I use your phone?"

The detective looked at him incredulously for a moment, then pulled out his cellphone, unlocked it, and handed it to Finn. His fingers trembled as he found the piece of paper Sarah had given him with their numbers and unfolded it. *Their numbers, thank God.* And the childish doodle of a head with a bandage plus the words: *Home care and pizza. Hanging House Special.*

His heart sank as his fingers fumbled over the keypad and twice he needed to start over until something clicked on the other end. "Come on..."

Her voice mail kicked in.

"No!" he shouted. It hadn't even rung. Dead battery? She switched off her phone?

Ignoring Detective Murray's wide eyes, he tried Emmie's number to the same result. No, no, no. Why switch them off completely?... Unless they intended to stealthily enter Hyde House. His heart beat faster and he dialed both numbers again while walking away from Detective Murray, leaving the same message to each. "If you hear this, don't go into Hyde House. Just get out of there. Grace has something to do with this. Zelda was doing it for Grace. I'm coming over."

He tossed the phone back to Detective Murray and began hurrying out, but the detective followed him.

"You look in a panic, Mr. Adams. What's going on?"

For a moment Finn stood confused, squinting toward a spectacular orange and red sunset. Any other time, he would have paused to marvel at the beautiful sight, but his friends might be in terrible danger. Wasn't all of this supposed to be over with

Zelda's capture? He spotted his car and lurched toward it, but Detective Murray grabbed his arm and held him back.

"Mr. Adams!" the detective said.

Finn strained for a moment within his grasp, contemplating breaking away, but calmed down and forced himself to relax. Better to not look desperate. "I'm sorry, but I forgot I have a very important appointment. I can't miss it." He pulled his arm free and ran.

"But the interrogation! She confessed."

"Great!" Finn cried, and never stopped. "I'll come back!"

As he drove by on his way out, the detective still stood at the station's entrance beside two other officers, all with arms folded over their chests. Finn would come back, but none of that mattered now. The only thing that mattered was Emmie and Sarah.

He pulled out onto the main road leading out of town and sped off. Forcing himself to keep below the speed limit, he calculated he would arrive at Hyde House in half an hour unless something unexpected slowed him down.

The girls would be there by now. "Dammit!"

As he moved along the highway as fast as he could, the photos of the victims, fresh in his mind from the interrogation room, came back to him. They had murdered each victim in a gruesome way, and he tried to piece together each case like a puzzle. That's why the law hadn't successfully caught Zelda until now: they'd missed the bigger picture. Zelda had been doing that for her mother like the Igor she was. The woman forced to bring coffee, treated like a servant. The decennial moon and renewal: *Keep Mama healthy and happy.*

Finn pressed the gas pedal a little harder as he sped out past the edge of town toward Hyde House. The pieces didn't quite fit together, although that didn't stop him from trying to make the connections. That old, frail woman, "Mama" Grace, would be at the house with his friends, no doubt, and she needed blood. Blood from young women. She had needed it the night before, when her daughter was already in custody; maybe she would try to get it today. Maybe young blood twelve hours later wasn't so bad. Good enough to perform whatever ghastly ritual she demanded?

He shivered, covered in cold sweat. *Sarah, Emmie. Get out of there!*

The image of a flower garden popped into his mind, and a sprawling web strung between some tall roses, with Mama Grace sitting in the web's center, like a giant black widow watching from the shadows. The girls might be hovering close to the web about now, drawn in by the sweet fragrance of the flowers and the tranquility of the garden.

He shook his head as if ejecting all the disturbing images. *No, they'll be okay. I'll get there in time.*

But arriving at Hyde House thirty minutes later, Finn's heart sank and his stomach churned when he spotted Emmie's car in the driveway, as well as another. The nurse's? Was she in on it too? Maybe he was panicking for nothing, and at any moment he'd see them come around the side of the house with wide smiles on their faces...

Don't kid yourself. Leaping up the steps to the front door, he found it ajar and didn't stop before rushing inside the house. Stopping in the foyer, he screamed. "Emmie! Sarah!"

He wasn't being clever about his entrance, but it didn't matter. If someone was hurting the girls at that moment, his loud arrival would stop them, although having a gun would have been ideal. But there was no reply for several seconds until a girl's voice called back to him, coming from somewhere near the center of the house.

Finn followed the source of the sound and hurried into the living room. The room was quiet and empty, and the gifts Emmie had brought for Grace days earlier now sat on the mantelpiece, carefully placed next to a framed photo of Daniel Hyde. Glancing down, he spotted the fireplace poker hanging from its iron holder. He didn't hesitate to grab it, holding it out in front of him like a sword, then continuing his search to a few locked doors before hearing the girl's voice again.

It was coming from behind him... No, beneath him. Turning back, he stopped at one door where the voice was loudest before opening it to reveal a staircase leading into a darkened basement.

He flipped on the light switch, although it barely illuminated the bottom of the stairs. "Emmie? Sarah?"

Another sound rose through the air. A moaning sound as if someone were hurt.

Resisting the urge to immediately charge down into the basement, Finn took a deep breath and held the poker out at arm's length, ready to strike.

"The police are on the way," Finn lied. "I'm armed, and I *will* freaking kill you."

28

The shock at seeing the dead nurse on the floor rippled through Emmie's body, and she couldn't move for a few seconds, even as Sarah pulled on her arm.

"Let's go. Emmie, let's go!"

Emmie finally turned away, and together they rushed back down the hallway toward the exit, but stopped at the sound of approaching footsteps. A door near them stood open. Inside was a long narrow room with sloping walls where the roof cut across it. It looked as if it hadn't been used in years, with the pillows on the bed perfectly placed and a colorful quilt covering the mattress. The queen-size bedframe was an antique; it might have been there since they'd built the house.

There was a sewing machine on a desk against one wall, surrounded by a litter of tiny doll outfits, many of them cut up into pieces. Strips of cloth lay nearby, and piles of small plastic dolls. They were naked, staring out across the room with wide eyes and outstretched arms as if waiting for someone to pick them up and comfort them.

This must have been Zelda's room. The psycho had left it unlocked like this?

The footsteps in the hallway grew louder, and they didn't

sound like that of an old woman's. They were swift and light, like those of a young one. Veronica? Was she back?

Emmie closed the door behind them and they dropped to the floor, scrambling to get beneath the bed frame. There was plenty of room. The frame was almost a foot off the ground, and within a minute they were situated and struggling to keep still.

The door to the room creaked open, and Emmie held her breath. She turned her head away from the door as the sounds chilled her. The image of the dead nurse popped into her mind, then the finger bones, then the dolls. Still, Emmie couldn't wrap her mind around it. Zelda was in jail, and the old woman couldn't be a threat—she could barely walk, let alone murder someone.

Someone else must be in the house... and we could end up like the nurse soon.

Emmie thought to face the feet of whoever had entered the room but was too afraid to adjust her position. The footsteps circled around the bed, and the shoes now came into view. The toes of the red nude pumps pointed directly at Emmie. Not the shoes of an old woman. They were those of someone much younger, someone who might be on their way to a wedding; polished, but outdated. Yet the woman's skin revealed her age. Blotchy, dry, and varicose veins running up her ankles. It could only be an old woman.

Grace.

A fight-or-flight response kicked in, but Emmie couldn't do either. Sarah gasped, although it sounded no louder than a whisper.

She has to know we're here, and if she's armed we won't have a chance.

A small object dropped at Grace's feet. About the size of a fist, a small twisted circular object made of twigs, cloth, and small bones that Emmie hoped weren't human. The sections were tied together by strands of hair to form an odd shape. The pattern laid out by the bones was clear: a pentagram surrounded by a circle. The same symbol someone had painted on her house.

Had this woman done that?

Emmie tensed and clutched her hands into fists, ready to lurch forward if she made any motion to attack them. If she grabbed the woman's feet, she could throw her off balance while they escaped. She couldn't imagine hurting an old woman—*they* were the intruders, after all—but this was no ordinary frail old lady.

Then, just as easily and nonchalantly as the woman had walked in, she walked out, leaving the pentagram lying on the floor in front of Emmie, and closed the door.

"She knows we're here," Sarah whispered to Emmie.

It was true. Emmie nodded, although the woman's actions baffled her. "After we open the door, make a run for it."

"Sure." Sarah's hands trembled.

They climbed out from under the bed cautiously, all the time keeping an eye on the door, and Emmie listened for any sounds of Grace's return.

Sarah gestured at the pentagram beside Emmie's feet. "Do you think she did that to your house?"

"Either her or Zelda."

"But Grace couldn't even take a step without Zelda's help when we were here before. She's almost a hundred years old, remember."

"Maybe it was all an act? Maybe she is someone else, or someone younger is wearing her clothes?"

Moving toward the door, the sunlight coming in through the unshaded windows darkened, fading in and out as the afternoon clouds passed by.

Emmie tried turning the antique glass door handle, but it was locked. She twisted it, then pushed and pulled, straining to open it without making any noise. "It's stuck."

"It can't be. I didn't hear her lock it." Sarah also tried and failed to open it.

A noise came from outside the window. Thunder and then pounding rain crackled against the glass. Emmie tried the door again, but it didn't budge. Grace, or whoever it was, must have locked it from the outside.

The white lace curtains surrounding the window fluttered as if a breeze had blown through the room, although the air was still and the windows were shut. *Just a drafty old house?*

Emmie stepped over to the window and looked outside. Storm clouds filled the evening sky and rain had swept in. She couldn't see much, except shifting shades of darkness. Wind rattled the glass as the remaining light drained away a little more each second. "This isn't right. We need to get out of here."

"How?" Sarah asked.

Pulling on the small brass handles near the bottom of the frame, Emmie tried to open the window. The metal was ice cold, and the air in the room had also cooled.

"I don't feel so good." Sarah stepped back and sat on the edge of the bed with her hands over her face.

Emmie hurried to her side. "What's wrong?"

"I'm sick. I feel... something evil."

The cool air sank through Emmie's clothes, and she shivered while rushing to find something to work the latch. A pair of scissors lay on the sewing table.

She jammed the tip of the blade into the door's lock. She doubted it would work as she turned the blade to the left, and was startled to hear a metallic click. *Was that it?*

She tried the door again.

It opened.

It couldn't be that *easy, could it?* She turned back to Sarah, "Get ready to..."

But Sarah was gone.

❧ 29 ❧

"Emmie?" Sarah scanned the darkness for any sign of her friend. Just a second earlier, Emmie was standing right next to her. She leaned down and searched under the bed where they had just been hiding. Not down there. She looked around the room. No other place to hide. There was a closet, but the door was open and the space narrow.

She went to the door and tried the handle again. Maybe Emmie had gone through it without her knowing. Sarah peeked her head out first when the door opened, just to make sure the coast was clear. She wanted to cry out to her friend, but that wasn't a good idea under the circumstances. It was impossible that Emmie would leave her there alone.

Still, there wasn't time to wait. Sarah glanced back into the room one last time to make sure she wasn't leaving her friend behind, then stealthily crept out into the hallway toward the stairway they had used before. She left the door open behind her, just in case she needed to make a dash back inside.

Several feet down the hall, she came to another door, which stood wide open. Hadn't it been closed when they had passed it the first time? Or maybe Grace had opened it while searching for them.

But there was a man standing across the room in front of a window—not the same window where they'd spotted him from outside. His presence startled her. The man's aura rippled over his spirit, defining his shape and size and features. He was a little taller than Finn, with a regal stance to his posture, and his clothes reflected the styles of the 1930s. This was the strongest aura she'd seen so far. He turned away from the window and stared at Sarah without any emotion. His expression changed to curiosity after their gaze met.

It *was* Daniel. His aura was just as she'd seen in his portrait, with the addition of broken lines across his wrists—the cuts he must have made when he killed himself.

Sarah stirred with excitement at his discovery, and she wanted to run and get Emmie, but she couldn't get anywhere without making a commotion and didn't know where her friend was. It would be just her and Daniel.

Somewhere downstairs, she heard more footsteps, but they were distant and fading. Maybe Emmie had gotten lost while looking for her, or maybe it was Grace, but there was no way to be sure.

Sarah stepped inside the room and closed the door, locking it behind her. She would wait inside and hide again, if necessary, but this was her chance to talk with the man who might have all the answers, even if Emmie couldn't be there.

Portraits of Daniel filled the walls of the room, and a man's hat and gloves sat on the dresser next to several neatly placed ties and cufflinks. It could have been a showroom in a museum demonstrating the appearance of a bedroom a hundred years earlier. There were even suit coats hanging in the closet and dress shoes lined on the floor directly beneath them, as if someone had kept them ready for Daniel to use at a moment's notice.

The open window behind Daniel revealed a beautiful sunny day outside. Could the storm have passed so quickly? Minnesota weather was unpredictable at best, but she'd never heard of it changing so fast. The beaming light brightened the room. Daniel kept his eyes on her as she stepped cautiously toward him, moving slowly as to not scare him away.

Daniel spoke, although no sound came out. His mouth moved, but she didn't hear a thing. Sarah leaned closer, straining to hear any words from him, but the only sound in the room was her breathing and occasionally the walls creaking.

Stopping a few feet away, Daniel let his emotions flare and his frustration rushed through her. His aura blazed in color between orange, red, and yellow. Whatever he was trying to say, it was important, at least to him.

Oh, Emmie, where did you go? This is what we were searching for. I need you here, now, to communicate with him.

Glancing around the room, she spotted a desk with a pen and notepad nearby.

"I have an idea." Sarah moved toward him, extending her hands toward him and passed through his arms, while opening herself to his spirit.

He didn't move away. If Daniel tried to possess her, like Josephine had done, she wouldn't hesitate to separate from him. She was confident she could escape any attempts to control her after having practiced it with Alice and studying Betty's books. This was Alice's brother, after all. His appearance and emotions resembled his sister's in many ways. His aura hovered like a rainbow in the air, a colorful fingerprint of his personality, his essence, that clearly defined his connection with the Hyde family.

Their spirits merged on a deeper level as she stepped closer. It proved as easy as what she had done with Alice. He didn't resist when she pulled on his hands, and she led him over to the desk, grabbed a pen, and pressed the tip to the notepad. As soon as the pen touched the paper, words flowed between them and onto the paper.

The handwriting was quite different from her own. His was

more fluid and clean. She sensed Daniel's delight in writing, and his spirit brightened as if he'd discovered a wonderful new talent.

Where is my Ruthie? Daniel wrote.

Sarah took back control of her hands while she answered him, but spoke out loud, hoping he could hear her. "I thought she was with you."

Not presently. She hasn't returned yet.

"Where did she go?"

A confused look passed over his face. *She's never far.*

"That's good."

Who are you?

"I'm Sarah. I'll help you look for Ruth, but I need to talk with you about Alice."

The connection between them abruptly halted, and the pen drew a harsh line over the page.

"What's wrong?" Sarah asked.

Daniel's mouth moved, but he bared his teeth as if cursing under his breath. He looked away from Sarah and his spirit went cold.

"Alice asked me to talk to you," Sarah pleaded. "She wants you to know that she misses you and wants you to come home."

Glaring at her, he grabbed control of the pen again. *Home? I'm home now. Alice died in the house she was to inherit. I failed her.*

"Yes," Sarah said, "she committed suicide."

A powerful emotion swept through Daniel's spirit. Grief. *The poor girl was very sick before that, dying a little more each day. How I agonized watching my poor Alice suffering at the hands of that debilitating disease. My heart died while she slowly fell apart, and I was unable to do anything about it.*

"What disease did she have?"

She was stricken with polio from an early age. Despite all our care, she became sicker once our parents died, and faded so quickly.

"Why do you think she became so sick?" Sarah thought about her conversations with Alice. The girl *had* said something about the strange taste of her food. "Do you think someone might have poisoned her?"

Who would want to poison my little girl? A preposterous and impossible suggestion. Ruth and I watched over her every day, and I would not have harmed a hair on my poor sister's head. The nanny also watched out for her and lifted her spirits, especially in her last days on this earth.

"I'm not so sure Alice intentionally killed herself."

Daniel's pain surged through Sarah. She felt his goodness and love, and allowed his pain to spill out into her body at the thought of his sister. As she gave up a little more control, a wail pushed up through Sarah's throat and came out loud and clear. She glanced toward the doorway. Maybe a little too loud.

She held back his pain and continued, "Do you know how the nanny died?"

She left town after she was no longer needed...

Sarah stopped his pen from writing anymore. It was taking too long to communicate. Opening the channel between them further, his voice rose in her mind. She could hear him now, although a little distant, like someone speaking to her through muffled ears. But his soft, low tone wasn't unpleasant, despite the intense emotional pain radiating from his spirit.

... and returned to her family.

Sarah shook her head. "We found her body buried in the basement of"—Sarah stopped herself before calling it Hanging House—"your old house in Green Hills." She pictured the woman's remains in her mind and winced. Her stomach churned at the thought of the tragedy that had occurred there. "Someone buried her behind a wall. She was murdered. Who could have done such a thing?"

That's impossible. The woman left town soon after Alice passed away.

"Did you see the nanny leave town?"

No, but Ruth escorted her to the train station in Minneapolis, so I know she was all right.

"She never made it there. Was Ruth ever mean to Alice or

the nanny? Do you think it's possible she might have poisoned them?"

Daniel's aura turned bright red. Pain flooded Sarah's head and her hands shook while Daniel scribbled out three words on the paper. *Take it back.*

Sarah struggled to regain control of herself as Daniel's rage grew. Alice had acted in the same way, erupting in anger after Sarah had made the mistake of accusing Daniel of malice, and now she had repeated the mistake by accusing Ruth without proof, but this was different. This time, she was sure that Ruth was somehow involved in the suspicious deaths of Alice and Catherine, although she didn't know the details yet.

"Okay, I'm sorry. I might have made a mistake, but I'm only trying to help."

Daniel's furious voice filled Sarah's head again. *Your mind is cluttered with deception and vile thoughts. She would never do such a thing.*

Sarah froze as an old woman screamed.

❦ 30 ❦

Finn descended the stairs cautiously. All the lights were on, but again the voice of a girl came through the air. It might be Emmie or Sarah, but if so, she didn't sound panicked. Didn't they see the danger yet?

The air smelled putrid, as if an animal were rotting beneath the stairs. *Maybe not so far from the truth.* Despite the light, there were plenty of dark corners and shadows along the edges of the room. The air was dank, and his stomach churned. He wanted to gag, but he held it back.

Reaching the bottom of the steps, he spotted a circle and pentagram drawn in red paint on the cement floor. It was surrounded by dozens of candles, none of them lit, and a book of matches. The red paint sickened him because he suspected it wasn't paint. He'd been right to rush back there.

He moved forward, steadying himself on the wall to avoid stepping on the circle and pentagram while still listening for any sound of his friends.

There was one door along the far wall, but it was closed. That had to be where the voice was coming from; maybe the pentagram was holding the women prisoner? The Lunar Stillness had come and gone, but could they have locked girls down here for a ceremony Zelda never appeared to perform?

It made no difference. He needed to get *everyone* out of that house, then let the police do the rest. Moving to the other side of the room, Finn spotted an assortment of sharp surgical tools, from scalpels to saws, and they were displayed on walls or stacked on shelves that encircled a small workbench. On a table, a variety of vintage syringes made of glass and metal, with needles of all sizes. He swallowed, trying to keep from heaving. He didn't need to spot the big roll of plastic standing on one side to know that this was the killing room. This was where Zelda had removed Natalie's blood and probably Jackie's; and she must have killed the other women farther away, in another state, so as not to draw the attention of local police. And God only knows what else they killed there.

As he moved along, he stopped near a collection of cloth voodoo dolls. Their style was similar to the one he'd discovered with the young woman's body in Emmie's basement and in his own would-be grave. Most of them were pinned through the head to a corkboard, and someone had dressed them in tattered, dark fabric and given them beady eyes. All of them wore a small necklace, threaded with pearly white beads: three small bones from a single finger.

His stomach churned. *I'm betting on the ring finger.*

Leaning in, he studied them more closely. Some dolls he didn't recognize, but others he did. One looked like Tommy's daughter, and three of them near the bottom rekindled his urge to throw up. No bone necklaces on those, but two were of women, unfinished, and one of a man with a large clump of hair that matched his own.

My hair. His doll was complete.

Panic swelled as he instinctively touched the amulet under his shirt. Had that thing helped him in the interrogation? No way to know, but it had better do something now. He stumbled back and forced himself to focus on the door only a few feet away. The back of his hair bristled, as if someone had touched him. He shivered, but stepped over to the door without looking back and turned the handle, gripping the fire poker more tightly and keeping it out in front.

Locked.

"Emmie?" he whispered. "Sarah?"

Someone whispered back to him beyond the door. The voice was murky, as if calling out from beneath something.

Or from within a coffin?

He pushed the imagery away as his heart beat faster. "Are you okay?"

No answer, but shadows moved along the bottom crack of the door. A faint light came from inside the room.

"I'll get you out," he whispered more loudly.

The wood frame was fractured and loose. If he pushed hard, it wouldn't hold him back. He leaned backward then threw all his weight against the door. The latch cracked open, and he stumbled into the room.

Holding up the fire poker, he ran into a wall of cool air and a flurry of hisses coming from a dilapidated ventilation duct running along the ceiling. But the other things in the room chilled him more deeply than the cool air. A blanket of human and animal bones, fabrics, animal skins, and occult artifacts hung from the ceiling in every direction. A pungent odor hung in the air, matching the revolting sights around him. At his feet, someone had painted another massive red pentagram with a star in the center, although no candles surrounded this one. No light in the room, and no windows.

She must have killed animals out there too, and performed her rituals here.

Something brushed against his cheek as he stepped inside. He flinched and wiped it away. *Probably a spider web.* But glancing to the side, he saw the long, thin, whiplike tail of a skinned raccoon dangling inches from his face.

Leaning away from the tail, he heard the voice of a girl again, now loud and alarmed. The muffled cries were coming through the air duct.

They're upstairs.

He turned and ran back toward the stairs, but as he stepped over the pentagram on the floor, he realized his mistake.

Too late.

The walls faded away, then the stairs. A paralysis spread through his body, and he struggled to move forward as the dirt walls began closing in on him. Scrambling to find a way out, he headed toward a nearby vent where an air duct hung low along the ceiling. He screamed for help at the top of his lungs, crying out for Emmie and Sarah. As the dirt pushed in closer, first swallowing his feet, then his ankles and legs, the candles surrounding the pentagram burst to life and the flames flickered brighter with every second.

An icy clutch wrapped around his body, like the vengeful hand around a voodoo doll. His chest tightened, and he struggled to take a breath. The dirt pushed in up to his chest, and the room darkened and squeezed him from all sides.

This can't be real.

He stared down at the dirt that rose inches every second. He focused on moving his feet, and within the darkness and dirt he could still see his shoes and the faint outline of the pentagram and the candles.

The dirt obscured his view again, but he kicked at the candles, feeling them topple against the cement floor next to his shoe. For a moment within the growing darkness, they were lying sideways on the floor, but their flames still burned brightly.

I've got to be hallucinating.

Is that you doing this, Mama?

Things were closing in around him, cutting him off from the outside world, just as Zelda had intended to do days earlier. Except now the terror rushed in along with the dirt and darkness. *She'll kill me this time.* Someone *will.* He gasped in a breath and his chest tightened. *Not enough air.* Opening his mouth wider, he struggled to heave in a full breath.

The shrinking room was looking more and more like it did when he was trapped beneath the ground in the crate, surrounded by worms and beetles. And that gopher had come out of his hole now. Back to watch him die this time.

His brother wasn't there this time, but Finn could hear his voice. *You're having a panic attack,* Neil said. *Focus. Get outside yourself and focus on your environment.* But the dirt kept rising. *Never mind the dirt. Just keep the air moving in and out.*

In and out.

The world lightened, just a bit, and Finn focused again, this time on the voodoo dolls back on the table behind him. He heaved in a breath and struggled through the thickness in the air, like trudging through molasses. Extending his hands toward the table into the thick blackness, he touched the three dolls that he knew belonged to Emmie, Sarah, and himself.

Scooping his doll up gently, he hesitated before ripping it apart. What exactly would that do to *him?* Would it have the same effect on his body? But he didn't know any voodoo spells to stop the connections to the dolls. He squeezed the first one in his fingers—the stuffing was almost certainly sand, by the way it shifted like a bean bag—and he felt a pressure against the sides of his chest. And what was it made of? Dirt from a grave?

He carefully unwound a small thread near the back of the doll holding the fabric together, expecting to feel his insides being ripped apart at the same time. No pain... yet he felt the tension against his spine. A few grains of sand escaped through the opening he'd created and spilled out over the table. Still nothing, so he poured it all out.

The suffocating soil and darkness stopped moving in, freezing in place around him as if the world had suddenly switched off.

Relief swept through him, but he cautiously glanced around. Would it start again?

Zelda couldn't be doing this. Not from so far away. It could only be Mama, and she was powerful, wasn't she, having done it for so long. It was her domain, after all. Her web, and she *knew* he was trapped and didn't need to be physically there to harm him. When he struggled, she could feel the web vibrating, fully aware that all she had to do was bide her time in the shadows, waiting for just the right moment to...

Just give up. The strange woman's voice seemed to come out of nowhere.

"I won't." He focused on Emmie and Sarah's effigies next, doing the same to them.

Hope that helps, girls.

But the void caging him in the room was still there. The stairs were somewhere... He strained his eyes to focus where they should be and walked blindly toward them with his hands extended before him. The thickness of the dark space tightened around him the further he moved toward the exit. Everything was still shrouded, and he grasped the empty space where he was sure the stairs should be, but... nothing.

It won't let me out.

On the ground a few steps away, the candles still burned, their flames piercing the darkness like devil's eyes, waiting for him to burn out before they did. He stepped on them, and crushed them with his heels, but they didn't go out.

Can't break the spell.

But I can shake the web.

He unpinned the dolls from the corkboard and lined them up on the table before turning over the first one in his hands to empty its innards. At least, it might help them. At most, it might disrupt the old woman's influence over them.

He carefully yanked on the thread sewn up the doll's back.

A woman screamed at the same time. Not Sarah or Emmie's voice this time, thank God, definitely an older woman.

Got your attention now, Grace?

The thrill of the small victory surged through him, just as

something shifted within the darkness. The dirt surrounding him shuddered as if a powerful force had acted upon it.

He tugged harder at the thread, but before he could finish the task, an invisible force yanked him back into the darkness. He lost his balance and stumbled back, clinging to the doll even as he crashed to the cold cement floor. The air rushed from his lungs as his hips, spine, and shoulders slammed down, then the back of his head. A flash of pain whipped through his skull and face.

His face warmed as he gasped the air in again and screamed. "Son of a bitch!"

What the hell had just happened?

But the pressure was still there, holding him down against the floor like a massive hand. It pulled his arms and feet apart until he formed a giant X. At least he was facing up, and he could breathe, but straining against the invisible captor did no good. It was controlling him like... a rag doll.

That amulet's definitely a fake, or the wrong god or whatever. No help at all!

Still, he refused to let go of the doll. And he'd dropped the fire poker on the floor near him, somewhere.

One of the lit candles was burning near his face. He turned his head to stare into its flame while catching his breath and calming his mind. Panic was setting in, but he wouldn't get out of this using force.

Below the candle, he spotted the edge of the giant painted pentagram and a few more candles burning around him. He was lying in its center.

Bullseye, Finn. You're right where she wants you.

A latch clicked above him in the darkness—the door at the top of the stairs. Then the faint sound of a woman's voice. His ears were ringing from the fall, and he couldn't understand her words.

But it was something like... "I'm coming for you."

"Sarah?"

There was no sign of her, even though she'd only been standing behind her a few inches a moment earlier. Emmie walked back into the room and searched beneath the bed and in the closet. She even scanned the floor for any trapdoors or obstacles that Sarah might have stepped behind temporarily. But she was gone.

This isn't possible. Emmie held her breath and listened for the sound of Sarah's voice.

A woman's scream broke the silence.

Emmie shuddered. Not Sarah's voice, an older woman's. Grace? The sound came from everywhere as it echoed through the hallway.

She hurried to the door as her heart raced.

Where are you, Sarah?

Emmie turned around and scanned the room behind her one last time before giving up and moving forward. It was impossible that Sarah could have gotten far. Had she become confused and run out into the hallway while Emmie was focused on finding her? She calculated the possibilities, trying to make sense of her friend's sudden disappearance, but nothing added up.

Still, she couldn't sit and wait for Grace to return, either. She stepped carefully into the hallway and moved toward the staircase. Passing the first door on the left, she turned its handle slowly. It was possible that Sarah had run to a different room, expecting that Emmie wouldn't lag, but the door was locked. Another door on her right was also locked.

Her heart ached to find her friend. She wanted to call out to her, scream at the top of her lungs, for Sarah to *GET THE HELL OUT OF THERE!*

But... Grace was near, and mobile.

Emmie walked further and stepped down the stairs cautiously, gripping the handrails and adjusting her weight to minimize the squeaky boards. It was an old house. No way to creep around without making at least some noise. At the bottom, she peered around the corner, expecting Grace to be standing there staring back at her, but the area was silent and still. Moving through the house, she spotted a window. Beyond it, an orange sky signaled it would be dark soon. Freedom was so close, but there was no way she would leave without Sarah.

She tiptoed through the hallway and checked a few more doors along the way. One of them opened into a small study room that had walls stacked with shelves of books, and another opened into a coat closet. The door to the bathroom where she had tried to contact Daniel during their earlier visit was a little further along. She opened one last door beyond that and stared down into pure blackness. The stairs disappeared into the darkness about halfway down. *No way I'm going down there.*

But a man's groan caught her ear.

Finn?

But what was he doing there?

He cursed from somewhere within the darkness. *Definitely Finn.*

She stepped down a couple of steps and closed the door behind her before calling out to him. "Finn?"

No answer. She found the light switch next to the door, but

flipping it on and off made no difference. The black air was thick, with no ambient light bouncing off the walls. Pulling out her phone, she switched on flashlight mode to move forward, but it only reached a short distance ahead. The darkness absorbed the light.

"Finn, I'm coming down." Emmie moved a little faster. "Are you okay?"

As she moved through the darkness, she spotted some small shimmering lights on the floor like twinkling stars. Leaning toward them, she realized they were flames attached to candles lying flat and smashed against the cement floor, although they still burned. A little further, she encountered a male form lying on the floor face up, his arms and legs spread out like da Vinci's Vitruvian Man.

"Emmie?" Finn couldn't even turn his head toward her.

The light from her phone illuminated an item in his hand. A voodoo doll. And a fireplace poker also lay on the ground a short distance away. Burning candles surrounded his body, which lay over a giant red pentagram.

"I can't move. It's Grace, but I can't shake her. Get out of the room, it's filling with dirt!"

She looked around, but saw no dirt. So Grace could manipulate the house as if it were a living being? Or at least create illusions in their minds, and this is how she and Sarah had become separated.

"There is no dirt, Finn," she said softly. Of course, Grace would use experiences they feared the most to prevent them from escaping. Finn's eyes were wide and sweat covered his skin, and her heart ached seeing him like that after all he'd been through.

He gestured with his head toward the floor. "Don't get too close. Stay out of the circle."

Emmie studied the pentagram beneath him. The magic had snared him like an animal in a trap. She dropped to her knees beside him, although stayed clear of the circle, and touched his forehead and arm. "I know it's her, though I don't know how." Emmie pulled at his arms, but some unseen force held him down. His skin was so cold, and he shivered and strained within the invisible bindings.

He groaned. "You shouldn't have come down here. We can't get out."

"Don't be silly, the stairs are right back—" She stared into the darkness. No stairs.

"We can't get to them."

"Sure we can." Emmie stood again and stepped toward the stairs. She could only get a few feet. A resistance pushed against her body like an energy field, so she hurried back to Finn.

He gestured to the voodoo doll in his hand. "I think she still has me under control with one of these little guys. Mine is up there on the table. I pulled out the stuffing, but it didn't solve the problem. I think I made things worse, actually."

Emmie stared at it, then scanned the table stocked with parts and pieces for voodoo dolls. She spotted several women dolls, each of them dressed in a miniature outfit, just like the doll they'd found with Catherine's body. All except three of them had their mouths sewn shut, and it was clear who the other three dolls represented. Finn, Sarah, and Emmie. That final step would have ensured their spirit's silence after Zelda had finished her gruesome tasks.

She looked over the extensive collection of parts and pieces. What did she know about voodoo dolls? Feathers were for protection. There was a bowl of black feathers in the back. Black was good too. Grabbing the doll depicting Finn first, she emptied the last of its contents, the smaller pieces Finn hadn't finished removing, and stuffed it with the feathers. Holding it up, she glanced back at Finn, but he still struggled on the floor.

It wasn't working. A moment later, she realized her mistake, and pulled at the clump of hair attached to the doll's head, slowly at first, to gauge his reaction. "Feel anything?"

"Nothing's changed." Panic filled his voice.

She yanked off the clump of hair all at once, like removing a bandage, and again watched his face, wincing and hoping she'd already broken most of the magic connecting them. Just that last piece left...

When the hair detached from the doll, Finn sat up suddenly, as if awakening from a horrible nightmare. He gasped for breath and looked around.

The thick darkness also left the room, fading away like a cloud, and the lighting on the ceiling brightened the room.

"Thank you, Em." He groaned again as he staggered to his feet beside her, rubbing his arms. He placed the woman's doll he'd held through the ordeal on the table next to the others.

"My pleasure." She gathered all the dolls together and studied them. "The high priestess was right. The hex is broken for you. If there are more dolls, there are more victims, and their spirits are probably trapped somewhere in this house. Remember how Catherine's spirit was connected with the doll in the basement? They can't be far."

"They look like the dead girls. Like Natalie, Jackie... And I've heard a girl's voice whispering and thought it was you or Sarah."

"I'll find them." Emmie closed her eyes. Only a moment later, a few vivid faces flashed through her mind. No need to pull them closer. The terror in their eyes was clear, and their voices rose in a chorus of cries for help. She opened her eyes and glanced around. "They're right here."

Finn glanced around. "In this room?"

The only door was at the back of the room, and she stepped toward it, grabbing Finn's arm and towing him along.

"There's not much in there," he said.

A woman's deep groan came from behind the door.

"You just can't see them." Emmie opened the door and a white, emaciated face jumped out of the dark.

🦋 32 🦋

Emmie froze. It was Donna, and the nurse's spirit was frantic to get her attention.

"I've got to get home." Donna shivered and lifted the hand with the missing finger. "I'm hurt."

Pushing the door open, Emmie saw six more young women in various states of distress spread out over the room. Natalie Cooper and Jackie Swanson stood among them. Their faces radiated fear and pain, their bodies were pale and gaunt, and all were missing their left-hand ring fingers, but another trait stunned Emmie the most: Every mouth was sewn shut in the same way Catherine's had been, except for the nurse's.

They must have killed Donna the night before, during the Lunar Stillness, when Zelda was still on the run from the police. Donna's killer hadn't bothered to sew her mouth shut yet, so she could speak. But like most murder victims, she didn't know what had happened to her.

Emmie moved into the room and tried to calm the nurse. "I'll help you, I promise. We'll get you out of here, but we need to find my friend first."

"Who's here?" Finn asked. "Who are you talking to?"

"All of them." Their icy hands passed through Emmie's arms

and legs as they reached out to her in desperation. "Come with me. All of you!" She rallied them to stand and move to the door, but they stood in place and shook their heads.

"We can't get out of this place. It's so cold in here!" Donna shivered.

The women's clothing was vastly different from one to the next. There seemed to be a different style representing every decade going back to the 1960s. A red-haired woman in a drab green dress looked as if she might be on her way to a college dance. Another wore a brown leather vest over a bright, flowery shirt and white bell-bottomed shorts with white boots, and hair that hung down to her waist. A blonde woman wore pink shorts with a turquoise blouse and tennis shoes with knee-high socks. A black-haired woman wore baggy pants and a short white top that showed her midriff. All of them looked to be about the same age, in their early twenties. All of them were exhausted, trembling, and terrified. And all of them had a large puncture wound on their neck.

Emmie's heart raced faster as they stared at her with desperate faces.

One from every decade.

Char's voice came back to her... *a treacherous day every ten years...*

The victims in that room matched the Lunar Stillness decennial, if Donna was the newest addition, but the killings stretched back even further than Emmie had realized.

But Zelda couldn't have killed them so long ago? In the sixties and seventies? Even in the eighties, she would have been young.

Emmie turned to Donna and gestured at the women. "How did you get here?"

"She put me here."

"Grace?"

But Donna seemed not to hear her question. Something near the stairway distracted her, and her eyes widened in fear as if some horrible thing was about to charge down the stairs at them. The other women had the same expression. Two of them huddled in the corner rocking back and forth, while the hippie girl paced the floor, clawing at her bloody hair. Natalie Cooper was struggling to climb up the back wall toward a section of patched concrete where a hopper window must have existed at one time. Another woman was shivering in the corner with her hands folded over her bloody chest.

"We need to hide," Donna urged, while pulling on Emmie's wrist. "Did she see you?"

"I don't think so."

"She won't let me go." Donna wept.

"We'll all go together."

The nurse shook her head and turned away. "No, we won't."

Emmie stepped over to Natalie. "Stay with me. I'll get you all out of here. Do you understand?"

Natalie looked at her with tired, pained eyes, but made no expression to show she understood. "She seemed so old, but she started moving so fast..."

Emmie returned to Donna who was now also pacing, running her fingers through her hair. "Listen to me. I'm going to take you all out of here right now, but I need you to follow me. Can you do that?"

Donna stared into Emmie's eyes. "I'll try."

Emmie gestured at the other women. "Can you get them to come along with us? They don't listen to me."

"Who?"

"The other women in the room."

Donna looked around. "We're alone."

She doesn't see the others. It wouldn't be easy to move them all out, but she wouldn't leave them there either. It should be a simple matter to guide them upstairs, even if they only got as far as the front yard, and it might be enough to separate them from whatever was holding them inside the house.

Emmie urged Donna to go first, but she stood in place with a hopeless face.

"What's wrong?" Emmie asked.

"She won't let me go." Donna extended her hand toward the doorway, but it stopped in mid-air as if pushing against an invisible wall. "There's no way out."

The dolls.

She turned to Finn. "Fill the dolls with black feathers, just like I did with yours. It'll break the hex."

"Got it." Finn nodded and went out to work at the table in the main room.

Emmie stepped around to each of the women, nudging them toward the door and distracting them from whatever trauma their minds had fixated on.

While waiting for Finn to announce that he had finished modifying the dolls, she couldn't help but think of Sarah. A jolt of panic flashed through her chest as her imagination churned up an image of what might have happened to her friend while Emmie and Finn were helping the victims in the basement. She pushed the disturbing mental image away as quickly as it came, but it rattled her.

"Finn?" Emmie called out.

"Almost done."

"Hurry."

Sarah's all right. She's got to be.

"Okay," Finn said a moment later, "done."

Emmie let out her breath and gathered the victims behind her, moving them all out the door one by one. Each of them needed to be led out with care, like frightened children escaping a treacherous cave, but she arrived with them a couple of minutes later at the top of the basement stairs. Pressing her ear to the door, she heard no sounds of footsteps or voices. "It's all clear now."

Finn had picked up the fire poker off the floor and held it ready as he stood beside Emmie. He'd shivered a couple of times along the way—every time a spirit had blindly passed through him—and he'd stayed off to the side.

Touching her hand on the cool brass handle at the top of the basement stairs, Emmie opened the door slowly and peeked out. All clear.

She turned back to the victims and stretched her hand toward each of them. "Just take my hand and I'll keep you safe."

They moved forward slowly with her, and she remembered all the frightened child spirits she had helped recently. These young women were no different. They'd been unspeakably traumatized and needed patience and love to guide them out of the pain and fear that blinded them.

Moving into the hallway, she focused on getting them out of the house, but she struggled with the idea of leaving without Sarah. The victims needed help, and so did her friend, but Finn couldn't lead the spirits anywhere.

Before she was forced to make a decision, a woman's voice echoed through the hallway. A familiar voice coming from upstairs.

Sarah's voice.

❧ 33 ❧

Sarah backed away from the door at the sound of the old woman's scream. It could only be Grace, and there were two options: run or hide. The mental image of the nurse's crumpled body flashed through her mind.

That could have been me. "We should hide," Sarah urged.

Daniel seemed to be in no mood to hear it. He still seethed from Sarah's insinuations about Ruth, and his anger radiated over the room like the harsh heat from an oven. But the scream had grabbed his attention, and the sharp anger directed at Sarah faded.

She scanned the room for a place to hide. Somewhere she could bring Daniel just long enough to get a few more answers. Then she would charge out of there and grab Emmie along the way.

Before she could do anything, Daniel stepped toward the sound with wide eyes. *My Ruthie?*

Sarah tried to pull him back. "We shouldn't go out there."

Don't be silly. Despite your outlandish accusations, Ruthie isn't someone to be feared.

"It's not Ruth I'm worried about."

Daniel showed a puzzled look. *Then who?* He didn't wait for her to answer before scoffing. *You're being childish. Let me take you to Ruth. I'm not sure where you discovered such awful stories, but once you meet my Ruthie, you will understand.*

"It's your daughter." Sarah watched the shifting colors of his face as she spoke. Would she upset him again? "She wants to hurt me."

He laughed this time. *Nonsense. Grace is a harmless child. Do her pigtails scare you?*

Sarah remembered the year of Daniel's death on his gravestone. 1934. Grace would only have been a little girl when he died, and it made sense that he would always remember her at that age, never having seen her grow up. "It's difficult to explain."

Daniel reached over, passing his hand through Sarah's. *You have nothing to fear.*

Sarah sensed his love again and relented. And talking with Ruth might yield more answers than with communicating with Daniel. "Okay, yes, take me to Ruth."

But never say these awful things about her again. She doesn't deserve such hateful words. Come.

Daniel's hand passed through hers again and they intertwined as he pulled her firmly forward. The cold, numb tingling reminded Sarah of waking up with one of her limbs asleep, but it functioned perfectly and didn't hurt at all. She allowed him control to lead her out into the hallway. Had the air gotten a little colder? Maybe it was just the interaction with Daniel's spirit.

Sarah moved along the hallway, entwined with his spirit. It appeared he would stop at a door on her left, one that she'd tried to open earlier, though it had been locked. Instead, he stopped at a built-in bookcase. The oak frame matched another bookcase beside it, but he piloted Sarah to push aside a row of books and unlatch a metal lock. The bookcase shifted slightly.

Daniel grinned at Sarah and held up one finger to his puckered lips. *Shh, I think my Ruthie is napping.*

Sarah's heart thumped in her ears as she glanced around the hallway for any sign of Grace. The woman had to be nearby—the scream could have come from the next room—and panic swelled with every second she stood there.

Sarah pushed the bookcase and the hair on the back of her neck bristled as it swung open a few inches. She held her breath, preparing herself for the sight of Ruth's aura, hoping she would see enough of the old woman's outline to engage with her. Maybe Emmie would still find her way back to the room wherever she had gone. But when the bookcase creaked open wider, the woman standing in the center of the darkened room wasn't who she'd expected. Yet, it was a familiar face.

Grace.

Sarah gasped and stopped breathing, unable to move beside Daniel's spirit.

Grace was standing unaided. But this was the same old woman who had struggled so much to get around the house during their first visit with nurse Donna's help. Now she smiled and rested her hands on her hips as if posing to meet them. With her head angled down, her eyes darted from one of them to the other, and she adjusted her polka-dot dress. *No, not polka dots— blood stains.*

Daniel stepped toward the woman while still connected to Sarah's hand, yanking her forward. Sarah held him back as the door creaked shut behind them.

The room was spacious with a coffered ceiling, and it was a giant shrine to everything occult and voodoo, judging by the objects on the shelves and hanging from the walls. There were clean skulls, both human and animal, and jars with hands, or teeth or eyes or bones or tongues, what looked like small, desiccated cats, statues of every size and shape, crosses and pagan symbols made of wood and twine. There were pentagrams made from wire and iron, and candlesticks perched on goat heads, daggers and candles of all sizes and shapes. On the wall, several hair braids of different colors hung, tied by string. Smaller jars had big labels saying: salt, long peppers, nitre, zimat, frankincense, *human* ashes. Big jars held all sorts of dried flowers, probably from the garden just out the back door. A musty smell filled the air, masking a deeper, underlying decay. Some of these things should have rotted long ago, yet somehow they'd been preserved.

The only light came from the dozens of flickering candles around the room. A giant black cloth covered the only window.

The other side of the room was different, much more what one might expect from the house. There were only a few pieces of furniture: two wooden chairs and a single long dresser that looked as old as the house. A white lace cloth protected the dresser's top from several carefully placed framed photos of Ruth's family. Hanging on the wall above those was a larger portrait showing Ruth and Daniel posing together with a baby held lovingly in her arms. Their faces clearly showed a deep love for each other and their family.

Sarah stared into the eyes of Ruth's photo. That was the same woman she'd seen above the fireplace during their first visit. Not Grace, but a young Ruth. Anyone could have mistaken them for twins. Their features were so similar.

One item in this schizophrenic, divided room chilled Sarah's blood more than anything else. A single wooden statue stood upright centered prominently against one wall. Its name was written in gold letters across the base: Erzulie.

A thick layer of freshly cut flowers circled the statue, and some of the petals had scattered over the wood floors, and jewelry of every type adorned its body, burying the statue's details beneath a blanket of gold and silver. Mixed in with the precious metals were an assortment of colorful beads and tiny stone carved symbols. Its feminine face stared seductively forward, the details of its exquisitely carved beauty nearly lost within the treasures.

One necklace stood out against the shiny metals. Shriveled, boney fingers hung from it in a jagged row, and they looked more like the long teeth of a predator than human fingers. But they could only have come from the victims.

And beside the statue sat a lone voodoo doll, charmingly dressed in a miniature brown suit and tie matching the style of the 1930s. A patch of brown hair covered its head. It stared back at her with lifeless, boney eyes. Masculine eyes, judging by the shape of them. No different from the other voodoo dolls she'd seen, except that this one was a little larger, and judging by the faded fabric, a lot older.

It could only be Daniel's doll.

Another short, broken wooden table sat at its feet, and on it were burning candles, a silver bowl filled with a dark red liquid, some of it spilled out across the table, and a wicker bowl stuffed with more beads, bones, and strips of cloth and hair. An offering bowl?

This is her temple.

"Hello, my darling." Grace stared at Daniel.

She can see *him.*

It was Grace, but something was very different about this woman. Something about her glowed. An aura spread out over her body like a mask, and the radiant beauty of the woman's spirit pulsed like a heartbeat in shifting blues, reds, yellows, and violets.

Sarah's eyes met hers for a brief moment, and a scowl stretched across the old woman's face before she again looked at Daniel.

"My Ruthie!" Daniel cried out. A wave of elation swept out over the room at the sight of her.

Ruthie?

Sarah searched the room for another spirit, and her mind reeled, trying to make sense of the woman's identity. How could Daniel think Grace was Ruth?

Simple.

Because she is *Ruth.*

The aura and the woman standing in the room were one and

the same. It was an aura of a young Ruth, the woman she'd seen in the photo downstairs, full of life and energy, shining through the old woman's body. The aura and body matched, right down to the deep wrinkles in the woman's cheeks.

But that was impossible. She did the math in her head. Ruth would be around one hundred and thirty years old, but this woman looked no more than eighty. Younger than she had looked when they first got to Hyde House. Still, Ruth's aura shined brighter and there was no mistaking the truth.

Inexplicably, Ruth was very much alive.

The woman's eyes glared at the overlap of Daniel's body with Sarah's. Her burning sneer transformed into bright red rage. "Get out of my Daniel!"

Ruth moved forward, extending her fingers toward Sarah's face like claws about to rip her apart. Sarah broke away from Daniel's spirit and stepped back. She felt the woman's intention to kill her, and one of the blood stains on Ruth's dress ran down and dripped to the floor—evidence that she could do it.

But her rage cooled when, with his arms out and eyes wide open, Daniel embraced Ruth's aura. She reacted physically to his embrace; she closed her eyes and swept her arms around him, passing through his spirit, and their entities overlapped.

"You look so lovely, my sweetheart." Daniel stepped back and looked her up and down, as she radiated more light than ever. Daniel looked at the covered window behind Ruth. "Should we go outside and walk beneath the trees in the backyard? Has the storm passed yet? When can we leave this dreadful house and go into the sunshine again? Remember our picnics with Grace chasing squirrels in the backyard?"

"I remember." Ruth calmed for a moment, then became more serious. "But the storm hasn't passed. Soon, sweetheart. Don't trouble your mind with the weather at this time. All will be well soon enough."

"Yes, my love."

Sarah moved around and stood near the side of the room

watching their auras interact. Ruth pushed close to Daniel, but glanced over at Sarah every few seconds.

To keep an eye on me.

Sarah inched back toward the door. It was open, and her muscles tensed, preparing her to run at the first chance of escape. How far would she get before Ruth struck her down with a hex? Maybe she was old and couldn't run fast, but this was Ruth's domain, and Sarah had stumbled onto the woman's dark secret. And Sarah couldn't leave without Emmie.

The photos on the dresser caught Sarah's attention again. "So you've been here the whole time."

Ruth didn't answer, only continued staring into Daniel's eyes.

"And Zelda is your granddaughter." Sarah stepped toward the dresser and focused on the smaller photos. "Is that a picture of Grace in the backyard next to Daniel?"

Ruth's youthful aura flickered with reds and yellows as a pained expression flashed over her face. "Little Grace..."

"Did you—"

"No," Ruth interrupted. "An accident. A horrible, horrible accident. The fire. I would never! Not her... Not my Daniel..."

"Just anyone not in your family..."

"They had a function." Ruth moved Daniel away from Sarah, stepping closer to the window and drawing his attention as she whispered into his ear.

"Then when Grace died in the fire," Sarah said, "you took on her identity, to hide your age and what you were doing here."

"I would do anything to be with my Daniel forever. I wish I could do more." Ruth stroked Daniel's hair.

"More death..." Sarah's voice trailed off. "Because when you die, you'll go to a different place than he did, won't you? Does he know?"

"He knows my love is eternal." Ruth pulled Daniel closer. "Don't you, my dear?"

Daniel swayed and swooned within her embrace. He, too, was hexed. Held to her by the ring finger bones stolen from dead girls. "I would do anything to be with you forever, my sweetheart."

"Zelda's been doing this for decades. Helping you hide all of this. Was it Grace before that, or you? How long has it been going on? Your granddaughter must have been so young when you forced her to start killing. You treated her like a servant!"

Busy caressing Daniel's arms, Ruth didn't answer.

"And you buried Grace in your grave. Nobody knew she died, except your family."

Ruth removed the black covering from the window and stared outside. Now their backs were turned to Sarah. The dark blue light from the setting sun did little to brighten the room.

The love was indistinguishable between them as they transformed into a single aura. Ruth broke her attention away from Daniel for a moment to glare at Sarah. Her face was full of anger, but also a longing desperation as his love encompassed her and drowned out all she had done. A moment of fleeting redemption for a doomed soul.

But even with Ruth facing away, Sarah knew the truth. There was no chance Ruth would allow her to escape alive after everything she'd seen. Even so, she inched back and prepared to run.

On three... one... two... three...

Sarah dashed to the door. And found her way blocked.

❧ 34 ❧

Emmie and Finn followed the sound of Sarah's voice upstairs until they located the source behind a bookcase, although the door leading into the room behind it eluded them.

Finn pressed his ear against the bookcase with the fire poker still in his hand and shuffled some books aside while Emmie stepped back and looked for a way to get past it. He crouched, placing the books on the floor, then turned to Emmie and shrugged.

Sarah's voice went quiet, and their footsteps seemed to creak louder in the uncomfortable silence while they explored the area. But she wouldn't leave the house without her friend. Sarah had to be in there.

Maybe she'd missed the door on the way over. Emmie stepped away from the bookcase and tried the nearby door handles, but all the rooms were locked. No way to enter them without making a lot of noise, but if that's what it took to get her out of there...

Dust rose in the air around Finn as he pulled out more books and ran his hands along the inside edge of the bookcase. His hands stopped on something and his face lit up. Nodding with a grin, he yanked some sort of latch until something metallic clicked.

The bookcase moved, just the smallest amount, as Finn set the books aside and pushed against it.

The doorway opened.

Stepping inside, with Finn and the spirits behind her, Emmie was met by Sarah's panicked face.

Her friend hurried toward them and waved them away. "No, go back!"

Emmie spotted an old woman next, staring at her from across the room.

Grace.

Emmie's heart raced as terror swept through her.

"What's wrong?" Finn pushed through the doorway, and he gasped.

But Emmie couldn't move. She couldn't take her eyes off Grace—because it wasn't Grace. It was an impossibly old woman appearing to be much younger by cloaking her aging body behind a ghostly, youthful mask, and Daniel stood next to her swooning over the charade. It was the woman she'd seen in the pictures around the house.

Ruth wasn't dead. There she was, alive behind the mask, orchestrating a tragic deception.

Not Grace at all. Ruth.

The moon: renewal. The eternal renewal of an impossibly old woman.

Daniel straightened beside Ruth with a bewildered expression as his gaze jumped from one person to the other. He could see Emmie, of course. "What's going on here? What are you doing in my house?"

Before Emmie could speak, Natalie moved into the room, passing through Sarah, and cried out in fear and rage. "She was there when the other woman murdered me! She watched it all happen, in this house, and bathed in my blood when the other woman dragged me to her feet."

Daniel could see her too! With wide eyes, he turned to Ruth. "What's all this, my love?"

Ruth scoffed. "Only mad lies, my darling."

Natalie moved over to a strikingly ornate wooden statue against the wall with the name Erzulie written across the bottom and extended her hand toward a necklace around the statue's neck. Several shriveled boneless fingers adorned the necklace, and she matched the empty space on her left hand to one of the fingers. She tried to touch it, but her fingers passed through it. "She has my finger on her necklace. I should have had a wedding ring on that finger someday, but she took it all away from me."

The blonde woman wearing bell-bottom pants spoke behind Emmie. "I see mine there, too." She faced Ruth and pointed at her. "You watched as that other woman forced me to kill myself." She ran her fingers over the puncture on her neck. "Do you think I would have done this myself?" She turned to Emmie. "Before I hit the floor, I saw that woman smiling at me from the shadows. She stood there and waited for me to die. And after my spirit moved out of my body, I watched her scoop up handfuls of my blood and wash it over her face like water."

The woman in the pink and turquoise outfit stepped over next to Natalie and also pointed at one of the fingers. "This one is mine. It hurt so much when she took it, even before my heart had stopped beating."

The bright-red spiritual bond Daniel and Ruth shared separated, and Daniel's expression changed to concern while he stared at the statue. "I remember when you bought this in New Orleans. You were so happy to have found the object. You said it was an antique and would…"

"… preserve our love," Ruth finished. "And it always will. But we can't let them come between us, Daniel. You have to trust me. You do trust me, don't you?"

Daniel stared at the statue expressionless. "… yes. But they…"

"… are liars, my dear."

Daniel leaned toward the statue, observing the fingers on the necklace. "How did I not notice these before? Is what they say true?"

"No." Ruth tightened her lips.

Daniel stared down into her eyes. "But what should I make of all this? Please tell me the truth."

Ruth opened her mouth to speak but glanced over at Emmie first. The woman's eyes burned with hatred. "The truth is, I love you, and we can't let them get between us, my love. Don't listen to them."

Daniel moved toward the victims and observed the wounds across their necks. "Who is the other woman they talk about?"

"Zelda," Sarah answered, "your granddaughter."

He furrowed his brows. "How can that be? My only daughter is eight years old."

Sarah shook her head. "You died in 1934 when Grace was eight, but she grew up and had a daughter named Zelda."

Daniel looked down at his wrists, then back at Ruth. "Yes, I remember now. I used my shaving knife to cut my wrists open in the bathtub."

Ruth shook her head. "No, never! You're alive. That's not true."

He looked at her curiously. "Little Grace stood in the doorway when they carried me out of the room, so frightened at what I'd done. And you promised you'd never leave me."

"And I never have, my darling. Almost a hundred years have passed and you've always been at my side, and always will be."

He nodded. "It's true, I killed myself. But how then can I stand here with you if I'm dead? What do you mean, a hundred years?"

"It doesn't matter." Ruth took his hand. "Forget everything they said, and we can continue like this forever, I promise. I'll make all the awful memories go away again so we can be like we were before. I can do it. You won't think such things anymore."

He looked over at the victims, then at the voodoo altar. It seemed like he could see everything. "What is all this you've kept hidden from me? Magic and witchcraft in the room we built for our children? You said you would stay with me forever, but... this?"

Ruth looked down. "I couldn't leave you. I had no choice."

Daniel pulled his hand away and stared at her until she looked up at him. "Please tell me it's not true."

The young Ruth was gone. Only a frail, elderly woman stood in front of Daniel, and she trembled while clutching her fists. "It was for us. For our family. Do you not remember when I lost baby after baby? All because we lived in that awful house with sick Alice! I begged you to take me away and you wouldn't. You cared more about her than your own babies!"

Emmie faced Ruth. "That's why you poisoned her food, isn't it? Then hanged her to make it look like suicide. Or did you hex her to do it herself like Zelda did with some of the women in this room? You must have been desperate to free yourself from the burden of caring for the girl!"

"I was pregnant again, and I wanted the baby to live. I wanted us to have a life!" the old woman cried hoarsely, tears streaming down her face. "His sister was doomed. She was doomed, but she was taking so long to die while my children died inside me!"

Sarah shook her head. "How can you blame a sick child?"

"And Catherine figured it out," Emmie said, relentless now. "So you killed her and stuffed her in a wall in the basement before you moved to the new house, to rid yourself of anything that might stand between you and your *family*. You wanted it all: his money, his children, his heart, and his soul."

Daniel had grabbed his chest and now shook his head as his eyes watered. "No. Not my Tiger."

"I lost that baby too, Daniel," Ruth pleaded. "Don't you remember what it was like? The third dead child? And I couldn't even conceive again until years later, but then..." Her face beamed once more. "Then we had Grace, our beautiful Grace. Here, in our house!"

"Alice!" Daniel's face contorted in anguish. "Catherine... How could you do such a thing?"

"And she enlisted the help of your little Grace for her evil," Emmie said, flanked by the ghosts of their victims. "And then of your granddaughter."

He glared at Ruth, not waiting for her to say anything. "You did, you did. I see it in your eyes."

Ruth spoke softly, staring without expression at the floor. "It's the only way we can be together forever."

Daniel stepped away from her. "I don't want that anymore. My heart is broken, to know what you've done. I see who you are now. I see you."

Ruth reached out for him, but he moved back.

"Don't look at me with disgust! Don't leave me, my darling. I'm the woman who adores you."

"Another lie. All this time..."

"It's still me inside." She pressed her hands over her heart, then dropped to her knees and clasped her hands together. "No, don't leave me, Daniel. My heart is breaking. I'm your Ruthie."

Daniel turned his head away from her. "Why did I die? Did I know this before?"

"I can make you forget again!" she repeated.

His spirit flared like fire and he screamed, "Never!"

Ruth crumpled to the floor as her spine arched and every bone protruded against her shriveled skin. The wrinkly texture seemed to worsen with every second. Her gray hair shriveled against her blotchy, white scalp. As she glanced up at Daniel again, all her loving features had transformed into the decaying face of a devastated woman, as if his fire had melted her.

Wobbling to the side, she crawled toward the voodoo statue and latched on to the silver bowl still full of blood at its base. With trembling arms, she lifted it above her head. But before Emmie could knock it away from her, it slipped from Ruth's fingers and splashed across the floor.

Clawing at the spilled blood, she smeared her fingers through it and wiped it on her lips. "We can be like we were. It doesn't have to end."

Daniel looked at her without mercy. "It does. It will."

A moment later, she toppled onto her side and heaved out her last breath, with eyes staring at the splattered blood.

Ruth's spirit separated from her body, black and churning, and hovered beside her until a larger swirling shadow appeared up through the floor like a black hole and swallowed it. The darkness faded until she was gone.

❧ 35 ❧

Emmie stared at the spot where the broken witch's spirit had disappeared. The woman had caused so much pain and death, but there was still work to do.

Sarah moved in beside Emmie and leaned against her shoulder. "I've never felt this much heartache."

Emmie wrapped her arm around Sarah's back. "At least, it's over."

Slowly, Daniel moved toward Ruth's crumpled body, now just bones and skin, and stared down with a pained expression. "I don't understand why I didn't see the truth."

Emmie inched up beside him. "It's not your fault. You couldn't see past the magic."

"Tiger... Yes, I knew all of this before. I couldn't stand the fact that I hadn't seen it in time and had not saved my sister. I was meant to protect her. Just a girl, and she had suffered so much."

"Tiger?"

Daniel smiled. "Tiger is the name I used to call my baby sister when she would storm around the house and fuss about everything. When she wouldn't get her way, she would growl like a tiger."

A memory of when Alice had done just that, chased Emmie out of her bedroom while making horrifying animal sounds, rose in Emmie's mind.

"I would have lived for Grace," Daniel said, "but her mother already had her spirit, I think. And I longed for Alice. I had failed to protect her."

"Alice is still there, you know, in the house where she died. Her spirit is there, anyway, and she talks to us every day. Most days. She's still looking for you, waiting for you to return. Catherine is there with her. I found them playing together in the attic a few days ago."

Daniel laughed. "They could keep each other entertained for hours. Catherine has such a wonderful heart." His smile faded as he glanced around the room and faced the young victims. "Please forgive me for not seeing past her deception."

"We don't blame you," Jackie said.

The victims had watched silently while Ruth died, but now they approached her lifeless body with apprehension. Their faces showed no joy, only relief and sadness.

Donna turned toward Emmie. "Can you lead us out of this horrible place? I don't want to stay here any longer."

Sarah stepped over to the nurse. "Let's do that now. It won't take long to get you out of this nightmare."

Emmie met Sarah's gaze.

Sarah nodded knowingly, then said in a tired, sad voice. "Psychics R Us."

"Oh, is it that time?" Finn asked, and moved to a chair. He sat down, looking exhausted. They forgot that he could only hear half the conversation, if that, and not see anyone else but Emmie, Sarah, and Ruth's bundle of bones and clothes. He'd been through a lot, but he leaned back, crossed his hands over his stomach and waited for them to finish, looking as solemn as he knew how.

Sarah faced the nurse first. The woman smiled weakly as Sarah approached her, as if understanding what was about to happen. Sarah closed her eyes, and within seconds the nurse's spirit shifted and glowed before rising and flashing away in a burst of light.

She did the same to another five victims. Then went Jackie, and the girls whose names Emmie didn't know. Sarah was getting good at it, with only a few minutes between each release, but Daniel and Natalie resisted their help.

Natalie walked over to the window and stared out. "Won't I get to see my father before I go? I need to say goodbye to him. He always worries so much."

Emmie nodded. "I understand, but—"

"Can you take me to him?" she asked.

Emmie pondered what Natalie was asking. *Not so easy.*

It was one thing to affect a spirit nearby, but Emmie hadn't pulled a spirit to her over such a long distance. Calling out to the little barefoot boy from Betty's basement had been difficult, but possible since it'd been only a few hundred feet. She could pull Tommy in, yes, but it might also pull in dozens of other spirits trapped in various states of distress, some of them even violent. It was all about the *focus*. But she'd been practicing what she'd learned from Betty's book about spirit manifestation. The process had interested her, yet she hadn't tried it on ghosts. A sort of "meditating and communicating" on steroids.

"Let me try something." Emmie looked into Natalie's eyes, then over at Sarah.

"What you have in mind?" Sarah asked.

"I'm going to bring Tommy here. It's not a matter of miles but of concentration. Right? And his heart is with his daughter."

Sarah's brows rose. "It's worth a try."

Stretching her hand to Natalie, Emmie felt the young woman's cold touch. She closed her eyes and focused on Tommy Cooper. Picking up on his spirit wasn't the hard part, as his face was still fresh in her memory. Within a couple of minutes, she'd calmed enough to sense his presence in the darkness, like a distant flame at the edge of her awareness. She pulled and strained to bring him closer. There were other spirits in the area, some of them dark and violent, and each entity responded, but one by one she let them go, for now, to bring Tommy in. It was just a matter of canceling out the distractions between them, like opening a radio channel and filtering away the chatter by adjusting the dials with great care. But the more she filtered and focused, the more she strained her mind and energy.

Natalie is here, Tommy. Your daughter is here...

There was a burst of light and a sense of wonder, and then Tommy came to her willingly from his house, as if understanding the reward at the end of the journey if he held on. His spirit still radiated the emotional pain from Zelda's control, and the wounds across his neck were still there, endlessly bleeding over his clothes and hands. But Emmie had him within her grasp, and she held his spirit in her mind like reaching into the depths of the sea and lifting out a prized fish with a fragile pole that might still break if she wasn't careful.

"Hang on, Tommy," Emmie said with her eyes pressed tightly shut. She moved him through the air, over the land and streets and houses and trees, and finally into Hyde House up through the floors to their room.

"Dad!" Natalie cried out.

Emmie opened her eyes just in time to watch them embrace, laugh, and cry together, although her head ached from the mental stress. They had no wounds on them now, only light.

"Good job, Em!"

Sarah took over and only a few minutes later both spirits swirled away together into the air.

Only Daniel remained with them. He had stepped over to the photos and now stared at the images of Ruth with a grim look on his face. "We all have to say goodbye sometime. It's time to move past all of this heartache." He turned back to Emmie and Sarah. "Please tell Tiger that I'll be waiting for her."

"I will." Emmie nodded. "I promise."

Daniel took one more look around the room. "You know,

when Ruth and I built this house, we intended this room to be a surprise for our children. They love special, hidden rooms, and we had planned to have many children to enjoy it. Look what it became. A temple of horror. I'm happy to leave now."

A moment later, Daniel was gone.

36

Alice's gaze was distant as she greeted the two women later that evening back in Hanging House, although she was close to the door as if she had been expecting them. She kept gazing off to the side, toward a spot against the wall, with an almost bewildered look. An expression Emmie had never seen before on the girl.

It was obvious Alice had experienced something profound.

"You saw Daniel," Emmie stated.

"No, but I can hear his voice. He's calling to me from far away."

"Would you like to see him?" Sarah asked. "I can help you go to him."

Alice glanced at Catherine. "I don't want to leave Catherine here alone."

"We can help her too."

Sarah approached Catherine. The stitches that bound her mouth shut were gone. No doubt, an effect of Ruth's passing.

"Do you want to go home?" Sarah asked her.

"I was going home. Now I remember," said Catherine. "It's been so long..."

"I know it has." Sarah reached out and touched Catherine's hand, tugging it gently forward. "It's not difficult. I just need to cut the cord holding you here."

Catherine held up her hand to Sarah, then looked at Alice, but the girl only smiled.

"I will see you soon," Catherine said. "It's just a holiday."

The tears in Alice's eyes made Emmie's heart ache, and her eyes watered up a moment later, but she discretely wiped them away.

Sarah closed her eyes and sent Catherine away in a flash of light. There was still a sense that Alice was holding on to the house, but only because she had feared to leave it, or have it taken from her.

She needed to know she was going home.

"Daniel wanted me to tell you something," Emmie said.

"What?"

"He told me to tell his Tiger that he would be waiting."

"Oh, did he call me Tiger? Where is he? Can you send me there?" Alice's tears streamed faster. Still, she growled playfully, just the way she had done to Emmie in her youth. It seemed that she remembered. "I hope I didn't scare you too bad."

"I forgive you. No need to say sorry. In a way... in a *strange* way, I think you kept me company," Emmie said. Better she say that than to say the girl had terrified her all the time.

"I wasn't going to say sorry, rube." Alice grinned. "Just take care of my house. It's still mine."

"Okay."

"You're so serious. I was joking; I know it's yours now."

Yes, she finally understands. "I'm just a little sad you're leaving, but thank you. I'll take good care of it."

Alice stared toward the wall again as if transfixed by something a million miles away.

Sarah said, "Would you like me to..."

"No. Thank you." Her face brightened as if she'd stepped onto a stage. "He's calling me." Alice's body dissipated into shards of light and rose into the air. It hovered for a moment above them, then flashed away toward the spot only she had seen.

In the silent stillness of the living room, Emmie cried, and Sarah joined her.

37

Weeks after the events at Hyde House, Emmie was idly lying in bed above her covers Sunday evening, too lazy for anything, when the sound of piano music came from downstairs. She imagined that Sarah was playing the song for Alice, just as she had done a lot in recent weeks, but reality came back. Alice was gone.

She glanced over at the music box still sitting on her nightstand. Alice wouldn't be around anymore to listen to it, and conflicting feelings swept through Emmie. It was great that Alice had finally found peace, but she couldn't help weirdly missing the girl too.

Climbing out of bed, she played the song on the music box, "O Sole Mio," even as Sarah's piano music continued below her. She knew the song by heart now and hummed along while getting dressed. Playing it so many times for Alice over the past months had filled Emmie with a strange sense of comfort—a peace in the house that she'd never experienced before.

A bittersweet quiet filled the room after the song ended, and Sarah's muffled piano tune gently played in the background. No more ghosts in the house. Just an empty, ordinary home now with a tragic past, but she doubted all the rumors and stories about the house would end. It would always be Hanging House to everyone in town.

She glanced out the window into the backyard. The sky was cloudy, but bright orange from the setting sun, and the bare branches swayed in the crisp autumn air. Dried, fallen leaves covered the lawn, waiting for Emmie to rake them up as she'd done many times before. So many memories filled the house, not only the disturbing ones from her childhood, but happy ones with her friends. It wasn't all tragedy, and she had grown a lot, not only emotionally but psychically. Just as her parents had always wanted.

Was it time to move on? There was still the problem of the history of the house. All the same issues were still there that her parents had run into when they'd tried to sell it once Emmie left for California. But Emmie could sell it with a clear conscience, knowing that the new owners, should she manage to convince anyone, wouldn't be purchasing a problematic home. At least there wouldn't be any spirits to bother them.

And if she sold it, could she and Sarah go live at Betty's house, the way Finn had suggested?

She brushed the thought away. Not important right now. She would wait and decide in the spring when she'd had more time to think about it. *Nobody likes to move in the Minnesota winter, anyway.*

Downstairs, she spotted the bowl of candy on the chair next to the door. Sarah had bought a large bag of candy earlier in the week intending to give it out to trick-or-treaters on the one holiday Emmie had learned to hate, Halloween. And even after Emmie had insisted that no kids would show up, except to prank them, Sarah had set the candy out on the chair. No kids had ever shown up on Halloween, with all the rumors surrounding her house, unless they were intent on causing mischief. But Sarah was the optimist in the group.

Plucking a piece of wrapped candy from the bowl, she ate it on her way to Sarah's apartment and approached her friend as she finished the song on the piano. Sarah hit the final keys and smiled up at Emmie.

"What song was that?"

"Alice Blue Gown," Sarah answered. "It's about a hundred years old, but still relevant... for us, anyway. I ran across the sheet music at a shop in Minneapolis. Do you like it?"

"Beautiful."

"Wish I would have run across it a couple of weeks ago. I would have played it for her."

Emmie paused. "I'm going to miss her, you know, especially after learning more about her past and everything she went through."

"She's at peace." Sarah stood up. "And we helped her get there, just like we promised. I'll miss her too." Sarah looked at the candy wrapper in Emmie's hand. "But don't eat all the candy."

Emmie feigned innocence and palmed the wrapper. "I'm sure you won't run out."

"We'll just see about that."

The doorbell rang, and they looked at each other, Sarah with a big I-told-you-so grin before bolting through the house to answer it. Sarah grabbed the bowl of candy, while Emmie opened the door.

It was Finn.

Emmie laughed. "Ha, I'm still not wrong, Sarah."

"What, no Halloween disguise?" Sarah asked him.

Finn stepped inside. "So sorry the cuts and scrapes all over my face and hands from the torture by witches are gone." Probably in defiance, he wore the same leather jacket Zelda had buried him in, and those rips would never come out.

Sarah poked her head out the door, and glanced up and down the street, then closed the door. She was hiding her disappointment very well for someone who always wore her heart on her sleeve.

Finn was holding his laptop in his hands. When he caught

Emmie looking at it, he grinned, then shook it in the air. "I got it back. Any plans for the evening?"

"Just a couple of witches staying home to study our craft." Emmie glanced back at some books in the living room.

"Good idea. Too many ghouls loose tonight. I passed a bunch on the way here."

"Headed this way?" Sarah asked, her face brightening.

He shrugged. "A few blocks down the street." His gaze stopped on the bowl of candy near the door, and he grabbed a piece without asking. "Shall we go to our office?"

They gathered around the kitchen table.

"You stopped by to tell us you got your laptop back?" Emmie asked.

"And some news," Finn said and opened it. His screen lit up and showed a news article with Zelda Hyde's photo off to the side. "Just in time for Halloween. Zelda confessed to everything and even led the investigators through the house and that horrible basement where she did all the killing. They found the bone trophies and hair and all that for a DNA-matching fest, and don't know what to make of the old woman's body, since they firmly believe it's Grace and won't accept Zelda's babbling about Ruth. Which is good for us, I think. I mean, the world won't suddenly all start believing this stuff, and we can just keep on doing what we do in the shadows."

"Our names got in the article." Sarah pointed to a spot further down.

Emmie cringed. "Oh, no. More attention." She read the first sentence on the screen, then stopped with a groan.

"Exactly. That's why the lack of belief from our friendly law officers is just great and should stay that way. And journalists. 'Unexplained, inexplicable' is better than them hounding us for details."

"So Veronica is at the house again," Sarah said as she read. "Hyde House. Super shocked and horrified, blah blah. Poor nurse, she says..."

Finn scoffed. "Yeah, right."

Immediately narrowing her eyes on him, Emmie asked, "You think she was in on it too?"

"Maybe not involved, but how could she *not* know? I've had a lot of time to think about this. I mean, especially when you're doing your psychic thing I sometimes have to stand there without knowing what the hell is going on for like, an hour—"

The two women exchanged an amused glance as Finn continued in his special smooth voice, "But has it occurred to you that the lovely Veronica was the one who set us on the path of discovery?"

Emmie thought for a second. "She told us about Tommy. And another voodoo murder..."

Finn nodded. "Instead of playing real dumb and not knowing a thing, she told us all about Natalie Cooper and sent us where we would discover more stuff."

"About her own mother?" Sarah's mouth gaped open. "Come on. I don't believe it."

"They didn't seem very motherly-daughterly," Emmie pointed out.

"No," Finn agreed. "But Veronica was very cozy with her grandma. Or great-grandma."

Working through the implications, Emmie spoke slowly, "So, she might have known about it all and... been an accomplice?"

"Why did Zelda have to be like the cleaning woman?" Finn asked. "She referred to herself that way, and we saw how Grace, I mean Ruth, treated her. And treated Veronica with admiration. Vanity is strong in that family."

"The beauty business..." Sarah whispered.

"Yep. And Veronica inherits all the crap in that house, too. It's not hard to imagine the old lady kept a tight rein on the magic and who could do what, had Zelda run around as her Igor maybe with some promises—but was really planning to hand the voodoo over to the young and beautiful Veronica."

"She said Veronica focused on life," Sarah recalled. "Something like that. But won't the police take everything?"

"The rotten carcasses and hair and bones, probably. But there could be secret stashes of knowledge somewhere, in another room hidden behind something or another. Veronica could already know spells by heart."

"Oh God." Emmie leaned back in her chair. "She is young now, but are you saying that, I don't know, some time in the future, maybe decades from now, there could be new bodies?"

Finn shrugged. "I'll be too old to care."

"Don't be heartless, Finn!" Sarah scowled.

He stood and gestured to the fridge. "Mind if I have a beer?"

Emmie shook her head. "Get one for me too."

"And me," Sarah added.

He brought three beers back to the table. "Nothing we can do now. Though I wonder what's in those creams she's making."

Sarah formed a concerned smile.

"But we're just worrying ourselves now." He motioned to his beer. "Time to move on and think about what's next. How about we all take a trip together? California? I'll pay. We need a rest before the next apocalypse..."

Sarah pursed her lips while glancing up at an angle. "Hawaii or the Bahamas would be better." She turned to Emmie. "What do you think?"

Before Emmie could answer, the doorbell rang.

All three of them jumped and looked at each other with wide eyes. Finn moved, as if ready to answer, but the girls scrambled to the door ahead of him. Sarah arrived first, after grabbing the bowl of candy with a gleeful squeal.

"Be careful," Emmie still said, "it might just be a prank."

But when Emmie opened the door, three children stood on the steps dressed in Halloween costumes. A young girl was a witch from a popular movie, a boy was caked with zombie makeup with plenty of bloody gore, and the youngest child, a girl not more than six years old, was dressed up as a princess. Each held out a plastic bucket in the shape of a pumpkin.

Only the youngest girl spoke. "Trick or treat."

"No candy for the witch," Finn said in a low voice.

Emmie elbowed him in the stomach.

"Oh, I love your costumes." Sarah liberally distributed the candy among the children. There was a car parked on the street with its engine running. Emmie waved at the shadowy figures within the car, and they waved back.

"You're awfully brave to come to this house," Finn said.

Sarah frowned at him. "Don't scare them, Finn."

"What do you mean?" Finn chuckled. "Halloween is all about the scares."

The boy's eyes widened. "I'm not afraid of anything."

"That's good." Emmie leaned toward him. "Always face your monsters."

They turned and ran back to their parents. Only the little girl called out, "Thank you!"

"Way to go, Emmie," Finn laughed after Sarah closed the door. "Weird advice from the weird lady in the weird house."

"Finn, you know where you can go."

"California?" he said while walking back to his beer.

Emmie turned to Sarah. "Wow, your optimism saved the day. I wouldn't have had anything to give them. Those are literally my first trick-or-treaters."

Sarah grinned. "And I'm sure they won't be your last."

Get the next book in the series on Amazon!
Whisper House: An Emmie Rose Haunted Mystery Book 4

Subscribe to stay in touch!

Get a **FREE** short story at my website!

www.deanrasmussen.com

★★★★★
Please review my book!

https://www.amazon.com/dp/B09BG4DJBZ

If you liked this book and have a moment to spare, I would greatly appreciate a short review on the page where you bought it. Your help in spreading the word is *immensely* appreciated and reviews make a huge difference in helping new readers find my novels.

All FREE on Kindle Unlimited:

Hanging House: An Emmie Rose Haunted Mystery Book 1
Caine House: An Emmie Rose Haunted Mystery Book 2
Hyde House: An Emmie Rose Haunted Mystery Book 3
Whisper House: An Emmie Rose Haunted Mystery Book 4

Dreadful Dark Tales of Horror Book 1
Dreadful Dark Tales of Horror Book 2
Dreadful Dark Tales of Horror Book 3
Dreadful Dark Tales of Horror Book 4
Dreadful Dark Tales of Horror Book 5
Dreadful Dark Tales of Horror Book 6
Dreadful Dark Tales of Horror Box Set Books 1 - 3

Stone Hill: Shadows Rising (Book 1)
Stone Hill: Phantoms Reborn (Book 2)
Stone Hill: Leviathan Wakes (Book 3)

ABOUT THE AUTHOR

Dean Rasmussen grew up in a small Minnesota town and began writing stories at the age of ten, driven by his fascination with the Star Wars hero's journey. He continued writing short stories and attempted a few novels through his early twenties until he stopped to focus on his computer animation ambitions. He studied English at a Minnesota college during that time.

He learned the art of computer animation and went on to work on twenty feature films, a television show, and a AAA video game as a visual effects artist over thirteen years.

Dean currently teaches animation for visual effects in Orlando, Florida. Inspired by his favorite authors, Stephen King, Ray Bradbury, and H. P. Lovecraft, Dean began writing novels and short stories again in 2018 to thrill and delight a new generation of horror fans.

WORD FROM THE AUTHOR

I took many factual liberties in this book with the beliefs and practices of voodoo for the purpose of building a better story. This isn't meant to slight anyone who follows their peaceful and loving religion.

ACKNOWLEDGMENTS

Thank you to my wife and family who supported me, and who continue to do so, through many long hours of writing.

Thank you to my friends and relatives, some of whom have passed away, who inspired me and supported my crazy ideas. Thank you for putting up with me!

Thank you to my beta readers!

Thank you to all my supporters!

Made in the USA
Las Vegas, NV
17 June 2023

73552662R00142